Dark & Evil

Compiled by
Brian Woods

To My Nichole –

Dark & Evil
Compiled by Brian Woods

Cover art By: Druscilla Morgan
www.amazon.com/author/druscillamorgan

Edited By: Brian Woods
www.amazon.com/author/brianwoods

12/10/2016

Copyright 2016 Authors©

Greg McCabe
Shane Porteous
Michael Lizzaraga
Mord McGhee
Jeremy Ferretti
Jeff C. Stevenson
Matt Shoen
Dawn Colclasure
Morgan Chalfant
John Kaniecki

Contents

Gateway to the Bottomless Pit
Greg McCabe

As Quinn rounded the corner, he could see his suspect sprinting down a long alley. Heavy rain continued to pour. The mass murdering bastard stopped when he hit a dead end—nothing but three un-scalable brick walls.

"Put your hands in the air, mother-fucker, or I will shoot you were you stand, so help me God!" Detective Edgar Quinn was a damn good cop, but he was also a mean as hell.

With his gun already drawn, Quinn took three large strides towards his suspect. On the streets and in the media, he was known as the Gateway Killer. He'd murdered at least fifteen people in bizarre and horrifying ways. There was always a bunch of satanic crap at the crime scenes: Black candles, severed animal parts, and all sorts of bizarre trinkets. Everyone said it was a serial killer, but Quinn figured it to be a group of people. In his experience, people that messed with that occult crap always did it in a group. It was probably some strung-out teenagers that had listened to one-too-many Marilyn Manson songs.

Regardless, just nine minutes earlier, a solid tip had brought him to a ramshackle apartment in the warehouse district. Quinn was standing at the door of the apartment, mindlessly looking at his phone, fully anticipating the lead would take him nowhere just like the dozens before it. Then a gunshot rang out. Instinct—not training—took over and Quinn dropped to the ground, covering his ears.

After a lengthy foot pursuit, he was less than a hundred feet from the person he'd been hunting for the last three years.

"I said put your fucking hands in the air, you bag of shit!"

Instead, The Gateway dropped to a knee and started messing with something on the street. Quinn holstered his service revolver and bolted toward his suspect. When he was less than a dozen feet away, the killer propped open a manhole cover and dropped inside. The detective made it to the hole just in time to see the Gateway jumping the second half of a metal ladder and splashing in knee-high wastewater.

Quinn had a decision to make: Wait for Wally, his rookie partner, or pursue The Gateway Killer into the sewer. It was really no decision at all. Detective Edgar Quinn holstered his weapon and began climbing down the metal ladder.

The detective looked down the seemingly endless concrete tube. He could see The Gateway turning a corner, fifty or so yards ahead and continued after him. Quinn ran along a concrete catwalk next to a flowing river of wastewater. His footsteps echoed loudly throughout the concrete corridor.

While the smell of feces was certainly in the air, the odor was not nearly as bad as he'd anticipated. His path came to an end and the sewer went two different directions. There was no more catwalk; he would have to wade through knee-high sewage just to continue.

But which direction?

He studied the passages. In one direction, the water was glass, perfectly still. The other direction, small ripples in the water rolled their way to the concrete wall and dissipated. He went the direction in which the water had clearly been disturbed.

The soupy wastewater saturated his pants and socks. He could feel slime mushing between his toes with every step he took. It was exhausting work. He could hear the sloshing footsteps of Gateway doing the same, just out of sight, in the sewers ahead.

After a few more minutes of disgusting foot travel, Quinn heard Gateway's footsteps go from sloshing to echoing, obviously he was out of the water and back on concrete. The detective picked up his pace.

Quinn made it to a rot-iron staircase that ascended from the sewage water onto a large cement slab. He found himself in a bricked room the size of a gymnasium. The corridor, like the concrete tubes, was dimly lit by large, caged light bulbs. He immediately realized that he was in the presence of people, a number of people. A quick scan of the room and it was obvious that he was in a hobo camp. Dilapidated tents and massive cardboard boxes lined the dirty brick walls. Filthy vagabonds went about their business, barely noticing Quinn's existence.

At the end of the large room was a three-way intersection of sewer tunnels. Quinn shined his flashlight down each one, unable to tell the direction the Gateway went. He located the closest destitute camper.

"Hey you, a guy just ran through here, he was wearing all black. Which direction did he go?"

The filthy old man with a matted beard just stared blankly at Quinn. Running out of patience, Quinn defied police procedure and drew his pistol, pointing it at the man. "Hey, dirt-bag. I asked you a question. Now answer it before I put you out of your misery."

An equally filthy woman stepped in front of him. "Please don't," she said, "he ain't right in the head. The person you're looking for went that way." She pointed toward the concrete tunnel that went right. Quinn put his gun away and continued without another word.

Thankfully, the sewer passage had a catwalk. He started jogging down it. After, what had to be a full mile, Quinn came to drop-off—a roaring waterfall of shit-water to be precise.

Quinn took a few steady breathes and looked around. He located a wall-mounted ladder next to the sewage waterfall. The flooring and ladder both descended into a miniature lake of waste water. He dipped his foot into the water, locating the next rung of the ladder. He went two rungs deeper, until the sewage was thigh-high. He poked his foot around, hopeful to find a floor. There was none. The ladder ran out of rungs when the water was chest-high. He was going to have to swim … through sewage … in the dark.

He took off his jacket and tie and left them on the ladder. He held his flash light and pistol in one hand and awkwardly doggy-paddled with his other hand. It wasn't pretty, but he was making progress.

About halfway across the corridor of wastewater, Quinn decided to turn on his flashlight in an attempt to locate the ladder he had previously seen on the opposite wall. As soon as the light turned on, the beam caught the familiar neon glow of a set of eyes perched just above the plane of the water. Quinn immediately believed it to be the Gateway Killer, waiting in the water to ambush. In another instant, he knew that it was not the Gateway, not even human.

The beam of his flashlight followed down the ridged back of an alligator. Its prehistoric body appeared to be at least ten feet long. Quinn's heart began to thrash. He drifted his flashlight across the water's top, noticing three other pairs of gator eyes, all staring directly at him.

He had no idea his heart could beat that fast.

After a few moments of fumbling, he was able to steady his pistol and flashlight on the closest one. This required him to tread water using only his feet, which was exhausting. His panting breath was becoming louder and louder. He hesitated as he noticed one of the sets of eyes had disappeared. Quinn shined the flashlight into the water around him but had no visibility in the murky shit-water.

He thought he felt something brush against his leg, it could have been debris, but he couldn't help but yelp like a frightened child. He thought about his wife, her beautiful face flashed through his head. He had to see her again. His story couldn't end like this—being eaten alive in a pool of shit.

He felt another brush against his legs. Terror consumed him. He yelled out and began to thrash about, dropping his gun and flashlight. In the same instant, he realized thrashing might attract the other gators. Without much thought, he decided to go completely silent and submerge himself toward the bottom. There was no rationale behind the decision, just blind panic.

He found the bottom and swam along it as fast as his body would allow while still attempting to be somewhat stealthy. He could feel chunks of god-knows-what hitting his face as he glided across the bottom of the cesspool.

He found, what he hoped, was the opposite wall. He groped around in an attempt to find the wall-mounted ladder, and by some miracle he located it. He worried he might climb into hungry alligator, but he had no choice. He was out of breath.

He climbed rung after rung until his head breached the water. Thankfully, there was no gator. He inhaled a much-welcomed breath of air, but it was unfortunately accompanied by the taste of raw sewage. He hastily made his way up the ladder and over the concrete deck at the top.

He turned back and looked at the lake of sewage, but it was too dark to make out any details. He was soaked head-to-toe in sewage, not to mention he lost his gun and flashlight.

Since he wasn't going back the direction he came, the decision-making process was simple. He would continue on, find the Gateway, detain him, and find another exit, surely there were plenty. At least he still had a pair of cuffs on him. *Goddamn, a gun would be nice*, he thought while double-checking for the revolver he knew wasn't there.

Thankfully, caged bulbs dimly lighted the bricked hallway ahead. He walked for what felt like a mile, each wet step reminding him of the toxic filth that saturated his clothes and body. He was disgusted and physically exhausted. He found himself zoning out from the monotony of the seemingly endless brick hallway.

Then suddenly, a door appeared. It seemed oddly out-of-place with its thick wooden panels and ornate metal hinges. Without readying himself or much thought at all for that matter, he pushed the door. It resisted because of its size and weight, but eventually opened when enough force was applied.

Detective Quinn was shocked to find himself standing in a well-lit, large concrete room. It was completely empty, except for what he immediately knew was an altar of some sort. Located in the exact center of the room, the rectangular table was also made of concrete and seemed to grow out of the floor—one continuous piece.

He noticed peculiar aspects about the room, like the fact that it was incredibly clean. Every inch of the room looked as it had been scrubbed with extraordinary care. There was also writing on the wall. It was in a language that didn't seem remotely familiar to Quinn. Maybe it was nonsense. Regardless, he marveled at its precise calligraphy. Clearly written with care, each letter was elegant and evenly spaced. The ceiling and floor were bare—clean enough to eat from.

After briefly exploring the large chamber, he found two small doors at the rear of the room. He opened one and entered a small hallway, having to duck down to do so. He was immediately overwhelmed with a pungent odor, like putrid eggs. He walked a little further and found another door. After sliding a bolt open, he opened it and was hit in the face with a scent so foul it made him immediately vomit. He tried backing away but slipped in his own puke. He tumbled forward, falling partially into the open door and the room that lay beyond it.

Quinn tried raising his hands and knees, but the ground beneath his hands wasn't firm. Rather it was some sort of gelatinous sludge. He was elbow deep in the horrid muck when he realized it wasn't mud his upper body was sinking into, but rotting flesh. With absolute horror, he realized the room was a corpse pit. A strained scream came from the back of his throat as he began to flail about. Thrashing only made it worse. The decomposing bodies seem to pull at him like quick sand. His face slid against the cold meat mush making him dry-heave.

Thankfully, his knees were still on firm ground. If his entire body had fallen into the room, he was certain he would have been suffocated by rotting flesh. Once he stopped panicking, it was relatively easy to work his torso out of the corpse pit. Before slamming the door shut, he took a quick look into the gargantuan room—barely recognizable body parts stretched as far as the eye could see.

Quinn made it back to the altar room and assessed his filth. He was covered in raw sewage and rotting corpse bits. His eyes stung and he was beyond nauseous. With great hesitation, he decided to try the other door.

It opened to a sudden drop-off, the size of an elevator shaft. There was a light at the top of the shaft, but it was quickly swallowed up by the darkness below, revealing no hint of a bottom. A thick rope hung from the center of the shaft, also disappearing into darkness.

Quinn reached out, grabbed the rope, and began sliding his way down it. He didn't even check if it would hold his weight. The exhaustion and toxic odors were making him delirious. He was operating like a lazy robot, just going through the motions, ready for a resolution of any kind.

He descended the rope until the lights above disappeared completely. Down and down he went. He hadn't climbed a rope since his training days. He vaguely thought about his career, which made him also think of his wife. His life had been going great lately, with a beautiful new wife and a recent promotion. These thoughts renewed his sense of determination and he continued down the rope in complete darkness.

He hit ground just about the time he was convinced that the rope would go on forever. After orienting himself, he noticed the silhouette of a door. Without hesitation or fear, he walked over and opened the door. It revealed a long hallway. As he walked down it, he noticed little rooms containing increasingly horrifying items.

The first room contained bones, shelves upon shelves of bones. Some of them were definitely human, but some of them definitely were not. He also noticed that they seemed to be meticulously organized. The next room contained countless vials of unmarked fluids. Some were as small as his pinky and others were the size of a mayonnaise jar. He didn't even attempt to imagine what was in them. Again, all seemed to be precisely arranged.

He heard terrible noises coming from the last room, high-pitched squeals and shrieks. Certain he was going to see people being tortured, he prepared himself for anything. Instead, he found animals of all sorts, in cages, scared at the approach of a person. There were goats and bats and possums and other creatures he barely recognized. They all wailed a horrible death cry. Quinn covered his ears and backed out of the room.

At the end of the hallway was another elaborate wooden door. He knew that whatever was in store for him was on the other side of that door.

As he got closer he heard a faint sound, a low humming. He stepped up to the door and put his ear next to it. It was actually a chanting sound. Although muffled, Quinn could definitely hear multiple people chanting in low, ominous voices. For the first time since his encounter with the alligator, he noticed his heart beating rapidly.

Weaponless and exhausted, he opened the door and walked in. There were a dozen or so individuals in black robes. They stood in a semi-circle in the center of a large room made of thick cream-colored stones. Every inch of the room was comprised of the same polished stone.

At a complete loss for words, Quinn finally said, "Which one of you sons-of-bitches have I been chasing?"

"Me," a woman's voice said from the corner. Another person revealed themselves.

It was the Gateway, dressed in all black. But a woman? He'd always assumed it was a man, or group of men. His confusion grew exponentially when he made out her face.

It was his wife.

"Jesus, Charlotte, what the fuck is going on? What are you doing here?" Quinn said, his voice quivering beyond his control.

"The reckoning is upon us," his wife said. "The prophecy has been fulfilled. The Gateway will open soon."

"What the fuck are you talking about? Gateway? There is no way you can be the Gateway!"

"I'm not."

"Then what the hell are you talking about?"

"You are," she replied calmly.

"You better start making sense or..." he trailed off realizing his threat was empty.

One of the robed figures broke from the semi-circle and removed the large hood that concealed all of their faces. It was Henry, his father-in-law, and the mayor of the city. There were even rumors of the smooth talking son-of-a-bitch running for president next year. What the fuck is he doing down here with this occult shit?

"I know you must be confused," Jack said. "But I think I can help shed some light on the situation." He walked toward Quinn as he continued: "We are all here because of you." The older man opened his arms and looked over his shoulders at the other robed figures, who in turn, removed their hoods. His confusion turned into shock and disbelief. His partner, Wally, was there, and his boss, the chief of fucking police. There were other prominent people, random world famous people that he recognized but couldn't put a name to.

"If you're trying to make things less confusing," Quinn said, "you're doing a terrible fucking job."

"Four years ago," Henry began, "the prophecy revealed you as The Chosen One. Since then, every single day of your life has been meticulously planned out to bring you to this precise moment."

"What do you mean?"

"I mean everything. Your promotion at work, your marriage to my daughter, the foods you ate … even the clothes you are wearing right now are all a part of the ritual of the Gateway. You should be honored you were chosen. Your name will live on for thousands of years to come."

Quinn took a deep breath and gathered his thoughts before speaking. "You keep saying chosen, but chosen for what?"

A smile crept across Henry's wrinkled face. "You are The Chosen One, The Dark Messiah … the Antichrist. The reckoning is upon us, and as our savior, you will act as the Gateway."

"I don't want any part of this nonsense. I don't know what you're expecting from me, but you're not fucking getting it. Besides, what exactly do you think I'm going to be a gateway to?"

"To the Bottomless Pit … the plane of existence that separates this world from Hell. You are going to open the gate and the Dark Lord is going to finish the war that was started when he was cast from Heaven." He bowed his head, "So sayeth the prophecy."

"You freaking lunatics are all going down," Quinn threatened. "You all got down here somehow which means there's a way out. I'm going to find it, then come back and burn this place down. If any of you are here when I get back, you'll be arrested … or killed for that matter—" He was cut off by a hand that was cramming a chloroform cloth over his mouth and nose.

A brief struggle … then … darkness.

Quinn awoke to sharp pain in his right hand and a loud banging noise. A man was hammering a giant nail through the center of his palm. The detective yelled out in pain. The excruciating process was repeated with his left hand. It wasn't until the man was securing one of his legs that he looked down and realized he was naked. Witchcraft looking symbols and letters were drawn all over his nude body in what he could only assume was blood.

Bang. Bang. Bang.

A nail was being driven through his right foot. Another agonizing yelp followed. Suddenly, he noticed the chanting again. He had no idea how long it had been going on, but it was mesmerizing. In unison, they bellowed deep, hypnotic tones. It sounded like words, but no language Quinn recognized. It was almost peaceful—

Bang. Bang. Bang.

His brief moment of tranquility was interrupted by another giant nail being hammered into his left foot. He looked around and to his horror, realized he had been mounted onto a giant pentagram—at least ten feet tall.

When Quinn looked back up, the semi-circle of satanic monks had closed in upon him. Their reverberating incantation was even louder. Inside the half-circle was a nude woman wearing a giant goat head mask. Or maybe it was an actual goat head. He could immediately tell the nude body belonged to his wife even though her face was completely covered by the bearded goat head. She also had odd symbols and pictographs drawn all over her nude body.

She began an odd dance as the chanting grew even louder. The sway of her body was enthralling, almost hypnotic. The pain in his hands and feet seemed to dissipate. Charlotte was handed a golden goblet, which she took while never stopping her dance. She walked up to Quinn and poured the contents of the chalice over his head. Warm blood ran down his face, chest and stomach, eventually making it to his genitals.

Someone broke from the circle and walked around behind the giant pentagram. They attached a chain to a latch mounted to the back of the configuration, then returned to their spot.

"Oh, Holy One," Charlotte said, her voice slightly muffled from the goat head, "Juggernaut of Darkness, we praise you in your highest as we bestow the gateway upon you. Make yourself known to this world as we bear witness."

Someone else broke from the circle and walked over to a device that looked like a medieval crane. The person turned a large metal crank and a series of gears started to turn. It eventually pulled the chain tight and began to lift the pentagram with Quinn's nude body firmly attached to it.

Two other people in flowing black robes walked over and pulled opened a large hatch in the floor. To his horror, the crane moved him directly above the opening in the floor and began lowering him into it.

He tried to think of something to say, but knew it was useless. He wouldn't give the satanic bastards the satisfaction of hearing him beg and plead. Lower and lower he went, until it was completely dark. He felt more strange fluids splash on his head and shoulders from above. The continuous chanting was still audible.

Suddenly, there was a rumble in the ground around him. A loud roar accompanied by a billow of hot air flew past him from some unseen place below. The chanting had stopped and turned into nervous murmurs. Something rumbled in the darkness below him. Quinn could hear its roar growing louder and louder. Whatever was down there was heading straight toward him. He couldn't bear to look, so he shut his eyes at the last second. While he could not see the beast, he could feel it passing though him—billions of tortured souls entering and exiting every pore of his body.

Suddenly, the nervous murmurs from the room above turned into terrified screams. Quinn was also scared, but it was not like the frightfulness he experienced as he initially chased a known killer through dark alleys. It wasn't even like the sheer terror that consumed him when he swam from the gators. He wasn't fearful of the intense pain he was experiencing or the fact that he would most certainly die in a dark pit. No, he was horrified that the occult people were actually right. That he was, in fact, the Dark Messiah.

Detective Edgar Quinn was scared for his immortal soul.

Apple Head

Shane Porteous

The air smelled of blood, as it should have, considering the fields were covered in corpses. Perhaps they had once been covered in long luscious blades of grass, or at least fine soil where grass could grow. Now the only thing that grew was the rancid smell of rotting meat. Instead of blades of grass, there were blood, bodies, bones and battle tools; all broken, all discarded, all dead.

Yagarva stood out amongst the fields, and not just because she was still alive or because she was bloodless. It wasn't even because of her garments, which looked like she had skinned a gray and gold spotted serpent into a suit. It was because of the dark blue cloth that wrapped around her head. Save for her short, sharp, black hair, the cloth covered her entire head. There were no cuts within the cloth for her to see, breath, hear or smell out of. But she did possess ears, eyes, a nose and a mouth, they could be seen under the cloth the way broken bones protruded but didn't pierce under skin. The cloth looked like a painful thing to wear, but painful in a perfect way. It seemed custom fitted to her head, the cloth the exact length it needed to be.

She walked through the fields the way a lioness lurked through the long grass, as if they were her hunting grounds, but she seemed far too scary to be a simple scavenger. The boots she wore were the same colour as her gloves, black and somehow beastly, like the material they were made out of came from the hide of creature too terrible to name.

She stopped then as she heard a sound that stuck out like laughter at a funeral. Someone amongst the bodies was still breathing. Yagarva had always been prowling in the fields, but now her prowling was focused. She approached the warrior slowly, seeing he had more wounds than weapons. There would have been a time when most women and even a few men would consider him handsome, but now he appeared as appealing as a ruptured spleen. His eyes were filled with blood, there was no white left in them, but his irises remained green as if the colour was powerful enough to protect him from being blinded by the blood. Yagarva ensured he was looking at her and thus knew of her presence before she approached, crouching down next to him so he wouldn't have to strain what little strength he had left to talk to her. His eyes fell across her frame, and not just because she was a woman and he was a man. He looked back into her eyes, or rather the cloth that covered them as he took another breath. It was small and strained, but it was now the most precious thing he possessed.

"I'm afraid I am going to have to request something from you," he said, his words as wounded as the rest of him. "Take what you want from my corpse, but please leave the letter in the sheath with me. It holds no value to anyone except myself and my wife."

In the same way he would've once been considered handsome, his voice was once noble and Yagarva could tell it wasn't a trained or tricked nobility, but a true one.

"I haven't come to steal anything from the corpses," Yargarva replied, in the same language but with a very different accent. It was as if the two of them were of the same orchestra, playing the same song but with two entirely different instruments. There was a darkness to her voice, it wasn't demonic or deliberate, but it was deep, like she had been born on a moonless midnight and had inhaled magical mist with her first breath.

The wounded warrior nodded, not so much in acceptance or agreement, but rather simple awareness as if, proud, he was still able to hear with so much blood billowing over his ears.

"You're a Bishbaarc?" he asked.

"I am," Yargarva replied with neither pride nor prudence.

Again the man nodded.

"You're a far way from home," he said.

"As are you," she replied, recognizing the symbol on the bloodstained steel plate that covered his chest as the mark of Massasis, a kingdom on the other side of the continent.

"That I am," he replied, still with simple awareness.

The next breath he took was smaller and sharper than the breaths that proceeded it, like sunlight weakening over the horizon.

"May I ask you something?" he said.

"You just did," she replied without cruelty or calculation.

"Then I will ask you something else," he said, taking her words as permission. "Is it true that in Bishbaarc there are trees so thick and tall that castles are built upon them, the way children build tree houses?"

"I'm afraid not," Yagarva replied.

The man nodded again, the green in his eyes growing with disappointment.

"Seems I wasted a trip," he said weakly. "That was the only reason I agreed to fight in this war. Thought I might come across a Bishbaarc that could tell me if it was true or not. I was kind of hoping that it was."

"I am sorry to disappoint you," she said, meaning every word despite her tone remaining melancholic. "The money wasn't a factor?" she asked, realizing that even noble men from Massasis could be mercenaries.

The man shook his head, his eyes closing slowly then opening quickly as he realized in his condition what closed eyes meant.

"It's the saddest thing about this world, if you have a weapon and know how to wield it, you don't have to travel far to find someone who will pay you to use it."

Before she could reply, his eyes fell away from hers, descending not in death, but to the dagger she held in hand. Its handle was white and yet somehow darker than her black gloves.

"No need for that," he said calmly, his eyes returning to hers. "I'll be dead soon enough, no point in risking damage to the dagger."

She glanced down at her weapon as if she had forgotten that she was holding it.

"Take my sword and sheath, but just leave me the letter."

She placed a hand on his shoulder, worrying not about the blood from his weeping wounds.

"This dagger keeps me safe enough; keep your sword, sheath and letter."

He nodded, his eyes not quite closing over, but they grew too heavy to remain fully open.

"I appreciate the favor," he replied, perhaps finally accepting she was telling the truth. That, or he had gotten to the point where he realized it no longer mattered. He honestly had nothing to worry about, at least concerning her. She despised thieves, liars and deceivers, hence why she was none of them.

"I could grant you another one if you like," she replied, her hand going from his shoulder to the small length of steel that hung from his belt. He didn't even look down at his knife whose handle was now in her hand, but whose blade remained in the sheath. He shook his head, taking a breath that seemed more painful than any of his wounds.

"The Gods of Massasis don't like it when warriors die from anything any than wounds in battle and as you can see the battle is over, the wounds I'm wearing will have to be enough." He then tried to chuckle, but the sound was more like a cough, cruelly plaguing him with more pain than he already had. "Funny thing though, I never really cared much for the Gods. Clearly they don't care much for me either."

If there was meant to be humor in his words, she didn't find it, as the green in his eyes grew distant. She had seen such a look before. She knew what he wanted; to see the face below the cloth. Not for carnal lust, but simply so the last face he ever saw in his life belonged to someone who still breathed.

It was a favor she wouldn't grant him.

He never actually asked, and his wounds were enough, the Gods of Massasis wouldn't be mad at him as he now passed into the afterlife.

She hadn't been lying. She let him keep his sword, sheath and letter, and she left his corpse in peace. That was the most potent thing about this place, despite the blood, the bodies and the battle that had bored both, the plains were at peace with what covered them.

She moved on, holding her dagger ever tighter as she searched the plains, still more like a predator than a scavenger. She only stopped when she found what she had been looking for; something one would think would be easy to find in such a place. There was a spot amongst the fields, a spot not covered in corpses or blood, at least not yet. Within the spot the ground was sloped, just enough to allow the blood to pool and form a puddle. She had come a few moments too early, the puddle was not yet formed, the blood was still stalking down the slope. From both sides of the inclined ground the blood flowed, tunnelling into a line on both sides, reaching towards the other like frightened children trying to hold hands in the dark. Yagarva couldn't shake the notion that both lines of blood were looking for a living body to flow into, but had settled on mixing with each other.

Yagarva crouched down before the lines of blood, like an explorer stopping to watch trails of ants finding each other and forming a new colony. Patiently she watched as the blood began mixing, forming a puddle several inches deep. She showed no sign of sickness, even though this blood smelled sour, like sauce that had gone out of date a decade ago.

When the puddle was formed it looked like a little lake of blood. Calmly she raised her dagger and placed it into the middle of the little lake, the way a child would place a toy boat in a puddle on a rainy day. She watched with her cloth-covered eyes as the dagger began to spin slowly amongst the blood but did not sink. She didn't take a breath until the dagger had stopped moving, pointing eastward. She shifted her head the way a weary camper does when they hear a howl in the night, before looking back at the dagger. When she was certain it would not move again she claimed the cutter, again caring not for the blood that now stained her glove. She had used the dagger the way a lost traveler uses magnetized metal in water to find north. She still prowled, but her steps were slower than they had been before, her head turning slightly from side to side ensuring no path in front of her remained unseen.

Mist slowly appeared to be moving into the air before her, but she did not stop and ponder its source. She knew where it came from, the same way only those who had been on battlefields knew what this mist was.

On cold days such as this, when warm human blood spilled into the air, the warmth would rise from the blood and bite into the cold, like steam rising from a freshly cooked pie. When enough blood had been shed in short enough of time, the steam would be so numerous it would form a fog, just like the one she was walking through. The dead bodies all around her now were the most recent dead. The final chapter in the book that had been this battle was now in her grasp. It was where the last of the fighting had occurred, where those too brave or stupid to retreat had finally fallen.

It was also where she was sure she would find what she had been looking for.

Moving through the mist she soon stopped, not because of another sound, but because of what she saw. At first he seemed only a shadow, crouched down, his back towards her. She was sure he was a man, his armor sat on his anatomy a certain way that was different to the way armor formed over a female. She knew the distinction personally. She took another step just to ensure the sight of him would shift from being a shadow to someone she could see clearly.

His armor was the same color as hers, like he too had skinned a snake to form it. His hair wasn't quite white, wasn't quite gray, but a color in between that flowed passed his broad shadows. The color had nothing to do with age, a lot of Bishbaarc men had whitish silver hair from the day they were born. Though crouched, he looked more perched, like a vulture carving into a carcass. She could hear him chewing on something and though she couldn't see what was between his teeth, there was only one reason for a vulture to carve into a carcass.

That is when he realized that he was no longer alone, his head rising the way a bear's does when they smell blood in the air. He then looked over his shoulder towards her, revealing blood between his teeth, blood that also covered his cheeks, blood that was not his own.

Bird like he turned his head back around and she could hear him licking his lips before he stood up. The action of his rising reminded her of a claw extending, ready to rip apart the world outside of its protraction. He turned to face her, the movement as morbid as blood turning silver in the moonlight. The first head she saw wasn't his, but the severed soldier's head he held in the palm of his hand. She had discovered what he had been chewing on, his teeth marks were evident where the nose had been torn off the face. Yagarva didn't find the sight of the severed head hellish; in fact it made her kind of hungry.

The living soldier had a face that could frighten frost off any surface. There was a graveness to his features, tombstone like and terrifying as if he hadn't so much danced with death but taught death how to dance. His eyes were the color of candlelight, orange and offensive. His chin was so sharp it could probably cut through stone. Yet despite the darkness of his features he was far from ugly, he was handsome, but there was something creepy about his comeliness, like he was handsome in the same way a house was haunted.

"Hello, Applehead," he addressed her as such even though he was the one holding the severed head like an apple. He didn't seem to speak his words so much as release them, like they were spiders and the world was their web. He sounded like the last thing you heard before you died and the first thing you heard after you were dead.

"Enomb," she replied, saying his name left a stain on her tongue, it tasted terrible.

He took another bite of the severed head, biting into the cheek and chewing slowly. Yagarva couldn't help but notice how Enomb's bite caused the head's muscles to flinch and its eyes to blink as if making the man alive again for a single sickening second.

Enomb swallowed before he said. "You're better than that, Yagarva," he began his teeth ready to become redder with another man's blood. "Address me as General," he told rather than asked.

"You're no longer a general," she told him.

"Aren't I?" he asked in a way that wasn't really a question.

He shifted his right shoulder slightly, making the insignia move as if marching to his command.

"You're no longer my general," she replied, smelling the fresh blood in the air, the way one smells recently made stew.

"But I'm a general nevertheless," he added, taking another bite from the head as if it indeed was an apple. Despite the cannibalistic chewing, his mouth rarely opened as he devoured the flesh, he was a monster, but a monster with table manners.

"Oh I'm sorry," he added, with a ghastly kind of genuineness. "Do you want a bite?" he asked, extending the head towards her.

Through the cloth he could see her eyes look down upon what he offered.

"I'm not hungry enough for that," Yagarva replied, knowing how hungry one had to be to eat a human head, she also knew what it felt like to quench that hunger.

Enomb nodded the way a crow nods after chewing on carrion. He then discarded the head allowing it to drop at his feet while he licked the blood off of his fingers the way one licks up sauce.

"Can't say I blame you," Enomb said, running his tongue over his teeth. "The flesh this place has on offer is sub par." He then smiled, revealing just how red his teeth were as if he was showing them off, the way a fisherman shows off his catch. "The heads back home were tastier than ham."

"I don't know if I would go that far," Yagarva replied.

This cannibalistic conversation was a calm one, like the two of them were talking about nothing more morbid than bread or breakfast. Enomb stopped smiling then and even though his teeth were hidden, he appeared all the more terrifying.

"No," he said darkly. "That was always your problem, you were never willing to go far enough."

"I've come far to find you," she replied, feeling her fingers tightening upon the dagger.

"Why is that?" Enomb replied. "Of what use would a general be to someone who no longer considers them a general?"

"Because you started something once that needs finishing," she replied, proving how dark her own voice could be.

Enomb then brought his thumb against his mouth, just for a second as if wiping away sickness. The fact he had been chewing on a corpse a moment before made the movement all the more morbid.

"If I started it, I should be the one to finish it don't you think?" he asked, wiping his thumb over his lips once more as Yagarva watched intently, not wanting him to reach for the sword on his back.

"I think you shouldn't have started it in the first place," Yagarva said.

In response Enomb straightened his back further the way a cat does before pouncing.

"That was never for you to decide," he said, his tone so cold, his breath actually added to the mist around them. "That was always your problem, Yargarva, you were … you are a brilliant fighter, but a lousy soldier. Soldiers follow commands; they don't question them."

"Soldiers fight other soldiers; they don't slaughter those who can't defend themselves," she said pointedly.

His head rose a little then, the action that of a predator. In that moment the mist around them actually began to move, like deer clearing from a forest where a wolf and bear would do battle. Enomb shook his head, a monstrous movement if there ever was one.

"How did it feel?" he asked, struggling not to smile. "I know you went to the Voltork Forest—that's forbidden—but you knew that."

When she did not answer he allowed himself to smile.

"I must admit," he began. "I always wondered about that forest. Is it true that the leaves are as gray as iron, curved like meat hooks, and the wind that blows through that place so powerful it can raise fully grown men into the air where they are impaled on those leaves?"

"I'm afraid so," Yagarva said simply, even though she was truly afraid of that place and she wasn't a woman who felt fear easily or often. "When I went in there men and women hung from those leaves like oranges in an orchard."

"Is it also true that when they scream, the sound summons demons and those demons dance to their screams as if they are songs being sung?" His smile grew the way a man's smile does when a beautiful woman is undressing in front of him.

"Yes," Yagarva said with the strongest syllable she had ever spoken.

The strength of her speech was strong enough to slay the smile off of his face as his features darkened, making the light of his eyes all the more bright and brutal.

"Sounds like a frightening place," he said as a man who did not frighten easily or often. "Tell me," he ordered, in a way only a military officer could. "How painful was it?"

When she said nothing, he elaborated.

"You went in there to get a worm, a deadless, I believe the old legends call them. Those same legends say that a deadless will eat the flesh right off your skull, slowly of course so by the time you realize they are under your skin it is too late to stop them. Then do they begin biting into your brain, like a worm through an apple? You'll have to forgive me; I can't remember how the legend goes exactly, but I believe the legend also claims the deadless will drive one mad. Yet, Yagarva, you must've already been quite mad to allow a worm to eat your head like it was an apple."

"I was mad," Yagarva replied, the words so weighty they were whispered. "But not insane. My rage was not only rational it was justified, considering what you did to me, what you made me do."

The words came out of her cloth-covered mouth like a growl, and for a moment her eyes seemed to glow like fire, although they didn't burn through the cloth.

"Does that cloth itch?" Enomb asked after several moments of silence. "Because that would truly be the worst part of your self induced punishment," he smiled humorously, revealing his blood bitten teeth once more.

"We all deserved to be punished for what we did."

"Did we?" Enomb asked apathetically. "So that is why you have come so far from your homeland? You brought a deadless to chew on my head? I'm afraid you're wasting your time. You see I know personally how bad tasting some heads can be, I wouldn't want to risk disgusting a deadless. Besides I already have been punished enough."

"No you haven't," Yagarva said sternly, sincerely.

It was then like a dead sun descending over the horizon that his smile shrank away leaving behind a night that was definitely going to be dark and long.

"Oh," he whispered. "Yes I have," the words left his lips the way steam leaves a kettle. "I was exiled from my homeland because of you, because of what you told the king; that weak minded fool forgot who we are, as did you!" He bared his teeth, going from being hungry to being a hunter. He wanted to kill something; not to eat, he just wanted something dead.

"I didn't forget. I never forgot."

"Yes you did!" he demanded. "We are Bishbaarc, Yagarva, it is what we do, we fight, we feed, we kill our enemies, down to the last man, woman, and child."

"Those people were not our enemies!" she bellowed back, her snarl so strong that the indents of her teeth could be seen behind the cloth.

"They gave shelter and food to Novvaks! Novvaks! The people that raid our villages and steal everything we work hard for, they deserved to die!"

"That wasn't your decision to make," Yagarva replied.

"You're right, it wasn't," he replied, causing her to ponder his words. "That decision had been made centuries ago, by our ancestors. The ones whose teachings are what we live by, it is why our kingdom and those who live in it are called by the same name, Bishbaarc, because we are one in the same! I will never see the shores of my kingdom again, but it is my kingdom, I am still Bishbaarc, as are you!"

"That doesn't make us the same. I never deceived you!" anger accented her tone, but so did disappointment, making her words all the darker.

"If I hadn't you wouldn't have done the deed," he replied slowly, almost sympathetically.

"Why did I have to do the deed at all."

"You know why, you might try to deny it, but you know those people deserved to die."

"No!" Yagarva snapped. "Why did *I personally* have to be a part of it?"

"Because," Enomb replied, sounding like a strict father disciplining his daughter. "You are a soldier and that was your order, I tried to save you from yourself."

"Is that what you did?" she replied with rawness.

"Yes," he whispered. "I took the hosvain, I placed it in your drink all so you would see those people for the monsters they truly were."

"They weren't monsters, they were defenseless villagers!"

"They were our enemies," he replied, coldly, calmly.

"You made me hallucinate," Yargarva began, her words biting at the air. "You made me believe they were beastly, hellish creatures and so I cut them apart. Then the hosvain wore off and I had seen what I had cut into, babies off of breasts, children out of their mothers arms, the elderly, the sickly, all slaughtered like pigs. You made me do it!"

"You're damn right I did, and I would make you do it again. You were the only one I had to use the hosvain on. The others knew what their duty was! You were the only one that would have defied the order, yet I was exiled because I used the juice of a forbidden fruit just to make you follow orders, and yet were you punished for it?" he asked, even though he knew the answer.

His eyes then glanced to the dagger she held in her hand, the one whose handle was white yet somehow darker than black.

"Speaking of forbidden items, that is the Dagger of Demnar...so," he added in a snarl. "That is how you found me? You followed the trail of battlefields, using the blood spilled under my command to make sure the dagger always pointed you in the right direction. Did the king send you? He wanted me dead? What? Was he worried an enemy of the kingdom would hire me to invade my homeland? He needn't have worried, the king is a fool, but I am still Bishbaarc. I wouldn't turn my back on my own kind … unlike you …" His voice trailed off like dying breaths, yet he remained as healthy as he was hellish.

"I'm not like you, or any of the others who were involved in the slaughter that day. You are all demons."

"What would you know about demons?" he asked, his words as powerful as they were petty.

Yagarva put the dagger into its sheath on her belt, the action reminiscent of a tooth being put back into the gum it had been punched out of. Her hands shook slightly as they reached up behind her head and removed the cloth in one motion.

When Enomb saw what was underneath he took a step back startled and he was not a man who startled easily. He couldn't really see her facial features, her head covered by a crimson that glowed the same color as blood. The light looked almost like it was coming from a lantern, lurking out into the world and casting bloody shadows. Enomb looked like a man who had witnessed a second sun rising from the soil like a zombie from the grave.

"What did you do, Yagarva?" He whispered, like a knife had been placed at his throat.

"What I had to," she replied.

Her voice had changed, sounding like she was speaking from somewhere deep inside a cave. It was like her head had been taken hostage by the crimson light.

Enomb brought his fingers to first his nose and then his mouth, wondering if the bloodstream of the head he had bitten into had been affected by hosvain juice. He had to be hallucinating. He moved to speak but that was before the rest of the mist moved, dissipating like sunlight giving way to the darkness. If blood mist was considered the day, he didn't want to know what was considered night.

"Everyone else slaughtered those people willingly, cut them up like cattle. They needed to be punished, you need to be punished."

Enomb looked back at the small red sun that sat between her shoulders. Wondering in what way was Yagarva about to change his world.

"But I couldn't do it; I couldn't hurt my fellow Bishbaarc, no matter how much I wanted to. But …" She paused and Enomb held his breath.

"They could," she said, raising her hands to either side and pointing at something that Enomb didn't want to see.

He saw them nevertheless. They looked like mini red moons that had moved from some sinister sky into the air all around him. The blackness grew darker and more solid, like a cave had been conjured all around him, a cave filled with red eyed fiends. He then heard a sound, like stone shifting upon stone, the sound of a mountain moaning; only this sound was a hungry one.

He looked back to the shining head of Yagarva, saying nothing, doing nothing. Within the crimson caliginous he could see them, if anything deserved to be called demons it was these creatures. Their skin was the color of wood, their monstrously muscular backs bristled with bony plates that protruded like weapons out of wounds. They were more hellish than any hell Enomb had ever heard of and he was man who had heard of many.

"For a man who claims to be a Bishbaarc you should have listened to the legends more closely," Yagarva said, her distant dark voice becoming black, like dusk suddenly shifting to midnight.

"The deadless are worms, glow worms! When they are finished feasting they use the leftovers like a lantern to cast this crimson light. It draws these demons in the way candle light makes moths move. The worms use the demons the way men use horses so they can get to their next meal faster."

His eyes wandered weakly the way a woman does after she has been raped. His vision moved across the monsters, they indeed were all staring at Yagarva like moths staring at a flame.

One second later that had changed.

Like morose mirrors of each other every head turned to look at him, their eyes glowing gluttonously, their teeth shining with salvia. It was as if Yagarva's mention of a next meal had made them hungry, had made them look at him. They stared at him the way he stared at a human head when he was hungry. They had feasted on Bishbaarc flesh before, Yagarva had made sure of that. All Bishbaarc that had followed his orders without question on that day had been dinner for these demons and he was the final course.

He had heard of vengeance, he had heard of retribution, he didn't know if this was truly either, but he was certain this was an evil act.

Finally Enomb moved, only then remembering the sword on his back. Before he could reach it, something stung at his fingers before they were severed from his hand and sucked into a demon's mouth. He screamed as he saw his fingers being chewed on, these monsters had no table manners. Before he could do anything else both of his arms were seized and snapped off his body like the legs off a cooked chicken. The demons weren't dancing but they appeared delighted by his screams. In a frenzy they feasted on his flesh, his armor no more an obstacle than the shell of a cooked crab. Through it all his eyes lunged back to see Yagarva. Finally he could see her features, or at least her smile, it was strong enough to be seen through the crimson.

Imagician

Michael Lizarraga

Acres of grass carpeted the hills of Hansen Park, embellished with bike paths and picnic tables, its vast view interrupted only by lush trees and restroom buildings. Cool October wind blew grim prequels of winter, the purple-black 10pm sky blanketed by L.A. smog and poked through with blazing stars.

Wearing sweat pants and a tight T-shirt, Shelley Holdridge mounted a sore leg onto a soda-sticky cement table bench for a hurdler stretch, a vigorous three mile run finally conquered. The picnic area was dim-lit by a nearby lamp post, giving off a yellowish medieval dungeon aura, while frog-sounding crickets conversed as if in a reed infested swamp, and the faint unpleasant smell of someone's remnant "weed" hung pungently in the air.

As the blond pony tailed woman stretched, she peered over the table and found a tall, frail homeless man wearing a dirty camouflage coat sleeping on the opposite bench, a scraped up acoustic guitar at his side. A forty-something gent with lengthy hair and beard, reminding Shelley of a Bible character, though his smell and snores were unholy.

The sneering jogger retreated before "Lazarus" could resurrect. Before he could ask her the infamous question she heard from people like him every day: Spare some change?

Roaches and bums, Shelley thought trudging up a grass incline. *Roaches and bums would be all that's left if we were ever nuked.* She gazed back at the snoozing guitarist as one would shoot a contemptuous glare at leeches.

The bearded musician was amongst many of Hansen Park's homeless "artists" that roamed the area, ranging from acrobats to magicians to painters who performed or sang or acted for cash. Like the landscape's trees and baseball diamonds, its homeless artists, too, were fixtures.

She put back on her earphones and turned on workout music from an arm-strapped smart phone, continuing up the football field-long hill.

Shelley, moderately pretty for a twenty-five-year-old woman, had a blank stone-like face that aged her and rendered her unapproachable. A persona of a stoic Dragon Lady, or the female cyborg from "Terminator 3." Even her boss, a former drill sergeant, always had a disturbing sense of dread around her, as if she was void of blood vessels or even internal organs.

But Shelley's "delightful" demeanor wasn't the only reason for her scowl this evening.

Three days ago, a good friend of hers was murdered.

Twenty-six-year-old Alan Mims was reclining in his Burbank apartment as usual, playing video games and smoking pot, when he was brutally stabbed by an intruder. He was found with a hole the shape of a sword through his chest and out his back, the Who-Why-How remaining as much a mystery as a brilliant Houdini act, the intruder taking nothing.

Alan was no altar boy, and often sickened people with his obnoxious attitude and slothful lifestyle, but Shelley knew of no one who would slay him medieval style. Aside from his pot and video game addiction, Shelley missed her friend.

Reaching the hilltop's plateau, the music stopped as Shelley's phone flashed its fifth low battery warning.

Shelley glanced right, to a small clearing several yards away, circled by cement picnic tables and thin trees. On top of one of the tables, silhouetted against lamp light and moonshine, sat Jasmin Morales, a tall Latina with long black hair and a voluptuous figure, wearing dirty sweat clothes and beat up tennis shoes. She was statue-still, facing the trees and brush, her back toward Shelley.

Since their freshman year at USC, Hansen Park had always been Shelley and Jasmin's point. Three mile jogs, two-hour tennis matches, a place to get smashed amid finals, a spot to pass out after parties. Although it was now two years since graduating – finals replaced with deadlines, parties traded for nightclubs, boys exchanged for boy/men - their Hansen Park refuge remained.

Tonight was an evening when Jasmin desperately needed Shelley with her.

Shelley approached the clearing, observing the silent woman who had not slept, ate or bathed for days, reeking of cigarettes and alcohol. Never one for sensitivity, this was all foreign to Shelley, and the Dragon Lady simply sighed. "'You know what's missing in this evening?'" Shelley quoted, hands on her hips, standing several feet behind Jasmin. "'That we don't have a very dry Vodka Martini with two olives in a chilled glass right now.' What's that from?"

Aside from being an alkie, Jasmin was an aspiring actress and an intense film junkie, often quoting movie lines and asking people, "What's that from?" Drove Shelley nuts. Nevertheless, Shelley hoped it would help wither away the gloomy storm cloud of a woman that sat before her.

Jasmin, however, was unresponsive, keeping her back toward Shelley.

Jasmin's boyfriend was gone. Alan Mims was gone. Dead. Killed a few days ago in his home.

They first met Alan two years ago during one of their typical Saturday morning jogs, the allured young man tailing closely behind them throughout their entire run, causing Shelley to blurt out, "Got some nerve, perv!"

They were Jack, Chrissy and Janet soon after, Jasmin and Alan eventually hooking up, Shelley always the third wheel. Although Shelley wouldn't have minded having the perv for herself, she figured he and Jasmin were a better fit. Jasmin was obsessed with movies and television; Alan was addicted to video games. Jasmin loved alcohol; Alan cherished weed. A match made in space.

Folding her arms, Shelley walked closer to Jasmin, who was still turned around. "Hey, girl."

No response.

Shelley's brows furrowed, a little spooked now. "Jaz? You okay?"

As Shelley stepped further, unfolding her arms, she watched Jasmin slowly and subtly get up from the table, fixated on something before her - something Shelley was unable to see, or hear.

Her back still facing Shelley, Jasmin stepped forward a few more feet, then stopped. Stood solemn, continuing to stare at the darkness before her.

"Jaz?"

Shelley's chest suddenly surged with shock at what came next.

Jasmin's entire head abruptly split in half, top to bottom, right down to her neck, as if it was a ripe melon sliced swiftly with a sword or machete—except … there was no someone with a sword or machete present. It sounded like padded leather or cooked turkey ripped apart, blood splattering and spewing along the grass.

Shelley's heart staggered while a tiny mouse-like squeak escaped her throat, observing the young woman's head halves dangling opposite from each other, a ghastly sight that resembled a giant Venus fly trap. The body involuntarily turned toward the wide-eyed Shelley, who now had a three-quarter view of the horrific half faces.

The insides simulated raw ground beef, and the entire display reminded Shelley of a child's plastic long-haired doll head that snaps in half and pops back in place. Or abstract paintings in waiting rooms or high school art classes. Or weird aspirin ads for splitting headaches.

The world went abruptly gray for Shelley and she wobbled like a three-legged chair, gawking at Jasmin's drooping, sagging eyes, the space between the head halves voiding a great jet of blood, almost solid. Shelley held on grimly, until the world swam back, watching the bloodied body sway and swagger like a drunken sleepwalker, then timber onto its back. Shelley unleashed an awesome scream, with great baritone bellows that splintered up toward wild Soprano levels.

She then blitzed from the clearing, bolted down the hill.

"HELP, SOMEBODY!"

Not a person was in sight; this area of Hansen Park a graveyard this time of night.

She reached the picnic area at the base of the hill, stopping at the table where she was before, the homeless man nowhere in sight. Panting, wailing, sweat minced with tears, Shelley ripped the phone off her arm, hoping for enough power for a 9-1-1 call. The drained phone, however, wouldn't even turn on.

Her mind whizzed along at mach two, like the last few seconds before puking on a wicked roller coaster, the discombobulated woman wondering what in God's sweet name just happened to her best and dearest friend.

The hell was she looking at?!

The hell could have done that?!

Maybe it's an abnormally weird condition ... causing a head to split in half under vast amounts of stress ... ?!

Bzzzzz! Next contestant!

Unleashing more hysterical sobs and shrieks, Shelley glanced back at the hilltop, waiting for her morning alarm clock to ring. Waiting for Jasmin to pop out any moment and yel,l "Gotcha!" holding a split-headed prop. Jigsaw-Jaz ... ha ha!

Sniper next popped into Shelley's pulsating head. With some sort of special weapon ...?

Shelley didn't feel much like finding out, and as her Mustang sat miles away across the park, calling her name, she prepared for another blitz.

Then she paused, a distant twig-snapping noise grabbing her attention. Her heart pounding in her ears, she gazed in the noise's direction, finding the homeless "Lazarus" standing several feet away in the lamplight, staring off into the distance.

Once seeing him with a flip-phone, Shelley decided on another 9-1-1 attempt, and scrambling toward him, shouted, "A girl's been killed!"

But the long-haired homeless man remained quiet and still.

"Hey! Hey!" Shelley yelled again, snapping her fingers at him as if at a dog.

He continued staring at something in the distance, eyes and face fixated.

Shelley faced the direction he stared in, finding nothing but trees and darkness, hearing nothing but leaves rattling dryly in a little puff of wind. Terror, directionless yet powerful, again flew through Shelley on dark wings, the man's behavior similar to Jasmin's before she split in half.

"What do you see?!"

Still gazing ahead, the man spoke in a mild tone. "What in God's name's he doin'...?"

Suddenly, a hole the size of a golf ball opened abruptly at the center of the man's forehead, blood spurting, the surrounding skin and flesh folded inward the way a small hole would open from a cracked airplane window in mid-flight. "Pwaaagh!"

With a shrill cry, Shelley held her face, fingers involuntarily digging into the soft pocket of flesh under her eyes as she watched the man's eyeballs roll upward, becoming bare white.

His jaw dropped like a draw bridge, arms dangled lifelessly, blood poured out of the head-hole and ran down his bushy beard like thin spaghetti sauce while he remained standing, teetering and tottering.

Shelley instinctively jolted back in anticipation to bail, but halted, mesmerized by something behind the man from a three-quarter view. Behind his head Shelley observed a long, thin line of blood and brain bits suspended in midair, as if covering a long stick, parallel with the ground and jutting from the back of the head, approximately one-and-a-half-feet in length.

While the blood dripped and flesh parts dropped, Shelley examined the "line" closely, her eyes bulging as she realized that the blood and brain were held up by absolutely nothing. Nothing she could see, that is, except the shape of some type of stick, blood forming a sharp triangular spearhead at its end.

An arrow?

Then the thin line of blood suddenly fell to the ground, along with the bits of brain, along with the homeless man, collapsing onto the grass.

Screaming, grimacing at the sprawled hole-headed corpse, Shelley was in half-shock, muttering in her orbiting mind, something ... captivated them.

The newspaper article on Alan flickered in her head: *Police baffled over man's mysterious death.*

Then Shelley's eyes caught a dark figure twenty feet before her, embedded within tree shadows and silhouetted against the yellowish lamplight.

It'll captivate you, too, Shell...

It was a man-figure, it seemed, his shaded outline replicating a shadow actor. His stature was thin and lanky, his appearance shrouded by the gloom, and all Shelley could see was a faint pale image of his bright clothing – a costume or outfit – consisting of a tight, long sleeve T-shirt and tight pants.

Close your eyes, Shell ...

His face was also opaque within the shadows with a kind of moon-like haze. His eyes – gleaming, beady, abnormally shaped – stood out the most, like cat eyes, or distant light houses.

CLOSE THEM!!!

But her eyelids would not even budge. Nor would her entire body, and she simply stood there, a mannequin with pulse, staring at the stone-still man. She tried with all her strength to move, but couldn't. The feeling was similar to sleep paralysis – waking up with a temporary inability to move, but it was something else. Another feeling, stemming from her brain, the cerebellum, intensely triggering her intrigue and fascination. The allure felt when seeing a car crash or a fight and unable to look away. Her pleasure sensors, the nucleus acumens, were also stimulated. A warm glow reminiscent to sitting in a soothing jacuzzi or bubble bath and not wanting to leave.

Slowly and steadily, the dark figure raised both his gloved hands slightly before him, waist-level, the way a weight lifter holds a barbell for bicep curls – elbows bent, shoulder width apart. He clutched his left hand into a fist, knuckles upward like he was starting a motorcycle. The other hand was palmed up, partly opened, as if resting something in it, like a "stick" or "bat" - and yet it was really nothing. Nothing but the vacant air before him.

All the while, Shelley struggled to close her eyes and move her limbs, her face drenched with perspiration. It was like trying to move through quicksand, or run for your life during a nightmare, and yet stuck.

His eyes on Shelley, his body remaining still, the man continued holding the virtual "stick" horizontally across his waist, the way a musician holds his guitar or a soldier harnesses his rifle. Then, with his right hand, he began touch/feeling another invisible device at the end of the stick, an object which hung from it like a flag off a horizontal pole. Gently, with precision and without sound, he glided his arched fingers over virtual curvatures, moved the hand steadily over the lengths and corners, indicating a large triangular, bell-shaped object with a rocker/smiley-shaped base. He then reached behind his back, withdrawing a smaller invisible object. He held it underneath the "bell," and began quick-stroking the bell's rocker base, mimicking a barber or butcher sharpening his tool, soundlessly, as if a T.V. set on mute. With his index finger, he gave a few silent "taps" on one of the object's corners to emphasize its sharpness.

Shelley, still attempting to move and close her eyes, was finally conscious of what was being created, and it was then the man moved forward, placing his right hand back onto the invisible "handle."

The man kept his "object" clutched at his waist as he approached, not a twig or leaf sound made from the ground where he walked. He stepped out of the shadows, now in full light.

His face was painted turquoise/blue, lips dark turquoise, matching his gloves that reached half his forearms. He was without emotion, cold, a sentinel or toy soldier, saying not a word. A ghastly laceration lay across his upper neck area. His left eye was abnormally huge, beastly, as if the socket harnessed a small baseball, shone bright yellow with a heavy vertical gash just above the eye and brow. His right eye was squinted and partially opened, as if punched or reacting to allergies, the eye color bright apple red. His black hair looked as though cut with a sugar bowl on top, bangs perfectly horizontal across the forehead. He was a terrific blend of KISS, Moe Howard and The Cabinet of Dr. Caligari.

More droplets of sweat ran down Shelley's neck as she conjured every ounce of energy to move, an intensity compared to an amateur weightlifter bench pressing his/her own body weight.

The painted-face man, meanwhile, placed his right hand at the end of the invisible "handle" with the other hand, raised both arms, holding up his noiseless virtual weapon like a ballplayer at bat. Just as the "tool" was in mid-swing, soundless as it flung through the air and a second from striking the shaking woman's neck, Shelley did it.

She broke free. Shut her eyes.

She anticipated the "contraption" crashing down on her, but it didn't. Nothing happened, as she stood there with sealed eyes, still feeling the strong grasp from the sensors of her brain.

As before, Shelley heard not a single footstep or movement from the man. Yet she felt his presence. Sensed his horrid face mockingly close to hers. Practically smelled his anger and outrage, waiting for her to break and reopen her eyes, like a lion pacing back and forth, anticipating its human lunch climbing or falling down from a tree, or a vampire in a standoff with its prey wielding a crucifix.

Shelley's body was no longer frozen, however, she kept her eyes shut, still feeling the seductive pull, and suspected she would still be vulnerable if she were to look at him. Her only option was to wait and see if this manipulative "spell" would eventually leave - along with him.

She stood there awhile, eyes shut, picturing him before her. Then, a feeling hit Shelley like an electric jolt, an overwhelming sense of familiarity about the face she'd just seen.

I know who he is.

Pictures flashed in Shelley's head. Flickers of the man, his ghastly face.

That mime. That stupid mime.

She and Jasmin would see him often in the park. That weird, grotesque man with the bright turquoise outfit, pantomiming. Anything from "walls" to "ropes" to "bows and arrows." Never once, as far as she could remember, did he ever speak.

Shelley and Jasmin paid him no mind, and like many others, no money. Not only were his performances trivial, he was a public nuisance. He'd follow people around, pester them to watch his acts.

After years of being shunned and mocked, the mime became worse, seeking retaliation.

He snatched people's hats and purses in play. Mimicked elderly and handicapped people passing by. Once he was beaten up for inappropriately close-shadowing a man's girlfriend from behind.

A hated mime. Despised. Ridiculed. Alone.

Homeless. For years, living out of an old abandoned turquoise and white ice cream truck parked along a public street near the park.

Dude, thought Shelley. *Dude the Mime*.

That was his name.

It had been a while since Shelley and her friends had seen him or his truck. Several months. Shelley had figured the freak-o moved to another place to harass others.

But what sort of "thing" was he now?

While she stood there in the frigid night, eyes closed, her skin flushed with primal fear from his ecliptic aura, Shelley was again jolted by something ... familiar.

The clearing. Its trees. The picnic bench. The bike path.

It all triggered a vivid memory, as if a re-occurring dream, or the way certain food or furniture smells can transport someone back to an old childhood den, or a pre-school or kindergarten classroom.

This spot. Right here. Yes.

It was six months ago. Before he mysteriously disappeared from the park.

Her eyes were kept closed, yet in her mind, they were opened. The gentle moon was replaced with a blazing sun. Stars became clouds. The cool air was exchanged for sweltering heat. Crickets were now birds.

It was one of their late afternoon jogs. Shelley at the helm, as usual, while Jasmin and Alan straggled behind. The "Alice Cooper/Marilyn Manson reject," as Alan refereed to the mime, was performing one of his stupid pantomime acts that actually looked kind of interesting, breaking the trio from their exercise. Wearing that turquoise outfit, that crazy make-up, unable to hide that hideous face: the grotesque eyes, the nasty scar, that ugly laceration on his neck.

This time, it was the costumed artist clutching his throat, beating his chest, gasping and panting for air, reaching toward Shelley and the others who stood before him.

Something new, Shelley thought. *A 'Help! I'm Choking' shtick. "Pant"-omime. Ha ha*!

"Lazarus" was also there, the homeless guitar player at his table strumming strings, watching the performer with little interest.

Still reaching out to the people before him, the mime mouthed words without sounds, his breaths becoming shorter.

He fell to the ground, onto his stomach, arms laid out as if skydiving. He lay completely still and quiet, his face turned toward Shelley's, his squinted red eye and enormous yellow eye glaring eerily at her.

A bit of clapping and a sarcastic "Bravo" from the three.

"Die, Mime!" Jasmin shouted, smirking.

Alan tossed him a dollar bill, saying, "Good riddance!"

Before joining her departing friends up the sidewalk, Shelley did a double-take toward the mime, catching something peculiar. Noticed purple bits of food embedded within green-brown saliva running down his chin. Several fruit dates scattered beside him, colored purple just as the food on his chin.

He was also a juggler, often seen bobbling balls, pins, or fruit. Once in a great while he'd plop something edible he was juggling into his mouth.

The "choking" act had looked real, too real, and Shelley had the sense something wasn't right. The mime's eyes remained open, gazing upon hers. Lazarus, too, had expressed the same awkward feeling. Stopped his playing, looked at the man, scratched his head. Then sleeked away.

Shelley had pondered the idea of staying, to see if it was more than an act, but she didn't.

Darkness shrouded the clearing as the sun turned back into the moon, Shelley's thoughts returning to the present evening, keeping her eyes shut while listening to the crickets and feeling the frigid night once again.

She stayed strong, the hypnotic grasp loosening, and she felt like "Alice" reverse-crawling out of the rabbit hole. Soon, Shelley felt no more pull, and slowly opened her eyes.

All she saw before her was his horrific yellow and red eyes inches from hers, jumping her heart into a gallop, and it was like gazing at an extreme close-up photo of the eyes of some wild animal, or like two blazing suns seconds from hitting the earth. She remained poised, matching his hard, unflinching stare. Proclaimed boldly, "We didn't kill you, freak-o, ... you choked."

You choked.

His turquoise/blue face remained before hers, inanimate, devoid of expression. Yet his big yellow eye began glaring slightly off to the side, as if mortified.

"Stupid mime," Shelley exclaimed, fear transitioning to anger. "What do you want? A hug? A big fat sorry?"

His dark lips remained closed, saying not a word, his yellow eye slowly shifting back to Shelley's, and she could swear that it welled.

Then Shelley watched as the entire entity began dissipating, as though fading into mist. Until nothing was before her except the dimly lit clearing.

"Ha!" Shelley blurted, wincing a half-grin, nodding in triumph. "Silly mime ... tricks are for kids."

***

Shelley, in her wind pants and Pink Floyd T-shirt, sat on short grass for a seated hurdler stretch. A crisp sunny day, birds chattering, Shelley's long hair gusting freely in the wind.

Encouraged to take time off work, Shelley had found this peaceful mountaintop "mini-park" for her workouts as an alternative to Hansen Park ... a place she will never return to.

Two weeks had passed since the "event." Shelley never told anyone what really happened, knowing a padded cell would await her. Instead, a Burbank business woman found her friend and a homeless man mysteriously maimed was the version for police and reporters.

Shelley did, however, find out some things about "Dude the Mime."

Recently, Shelley had spotted a shirtless street dancer performing at a gas station near Hansen Park. Recognizing the fifty-something homeless man from the park, Shelley discretely asked if he'd known the mime. Continuing his Michael Jackson rendition while playing "PYT," the former semi-pro baseball player reluctantly obliged Shelley.

Ten years ago, Nelson "Dude" Rucker was a stand-up comic on his way to stardom, but Nelson was also involved with certain "business associates" and was found one day in an alley with a deformed face and his vocal cords surgically severed from his throat.

No longer able to perform on stage, no longer able to support his family, his wife left him, taking their five-year-old son. Nelson had no place but the streets, and had been there ever since, miming for money. Like many homeless people, the streets got to him, and he gradually became mentally ill.

"Guess you can say that crazy clown had gagged himself out of his own misery," the dancer had punned as Shelley left the gas station.

Shelley glanced up from her stretch, looked at the other side of the grass field. Thirty feet away sat a woman in a wheelchair who resembled a creature as old as time, pushed by a young man parking the chair so she could enjoy the view.

Her body was a scrawny stick, shoulders hunched almost to the back of her skull. She wore a pink nightgown, had snow white hair put in a bun, and slack and droopy prune-like skin.

Her cheekbones were incredibly high, her half-lidded eyes burrowed into her face. Her firm, thin lips cast not a smile, nor a frown.

The man gave the old woman gentle back pats, whispering in her ear. Not only did the woman seem oblivious to the man, but to the entire world around her, and simply stared straight ahead. Then the caregiver walked away, likely for a cigarette or bathroom break.

As she stretched, Shelley thought about Jasmin, as she often did since that night. She reflected on their times in college. Friday nights at "The Crave." Jasmin's dumb movie trivia.

She reflected on Alan. Remembered their hot little "thaing" together before he and Jasmin dated—okay, once while they dated, but only once.

She missed her friends. Wished they would have been stronger, like her.

Victims of that "Mad Hatter's" rabbit hole, thought Shelley. That fantasy escape chute for the weak minded and weak willed. That hole for users, drinkers, gamblers, spenders, eaters, gamers, internet addicts, couch veggies, porn junkies, lottery players, horoscope readers, idol worshipers and bums.

But that hole is not for you, Shell ... not for you.

Shelley gazed up, noticed the old woman staring in her direction. Not directly at Shelley, but around her, the woman now having a slight grin, as if given some pudding or Jell-O. Shelley hated being stared at, especially by kids and old people. It irked her, the way people get irritated by someone chewing with their mouth opened.

Shelley got up from the grass, the woman's annoying stares being her cue to leave. She stepped no more than two feet before she was abruptly stopped in her tracks.

"Nuuugh!" she shrieked.

It was as if Shelley walked straight into a wall with her cheekbone and shoulder, and as she instinctively touched her cheek, she realized there was no pain. More stunningly, there was no sight, nor sound of whatever it was she walked into.

"Whaa...?"

Shelley put her hand out before her. With four fingers, she touched something. A barrier, a force of some kind. She placed both her palms vertically against the barrier with a bit more pressure. It felt neither hard, nor soft, and it made not a single sound as she touched it. An invisible, noiseless barrier, as though touching tremendous wind or water pressure powerful enough to stop anything – without there being any sort of wind or water.

Shelley glanced at the old woman, who now stared at her with a bigger smile, the way she might have once watched her grandchildren playing in sand.

Shelley slid her right palm along the invisible "wall," a foot and a half to her right, her hand stopped by another invisible barrier. Facing this wall, she slid the same palm along the mysterious barrier, to the right, and after three feet, reached another wall. She repeated the pattern, palming two more walls, each thee feet wide, until she was back where she started.

"Oh...my...God..."

It was a transparent "box," the size of a phone booth, and after several more feels, she found that the invisible "walls" reached from the ground up above her head. As though surrounded by highly spotless glass doors – yet not. She still heard bird chirps, felt cool breeze, watched a squirrel enter and exit past one of the walls. The box was nonresistant to light, sound, and objects – except Shelley.

Then it occurred to Shelley's overloaded mind like a light on the horizon. She looked around the grass field, through her invisible "cage." No sign of him anywhere.

Has to be him.

But he's gotta be seen for his tricks to work.

She also felt no stern seductive pull within her cerebellum, on her nerves or in her muscles, and wondered how this was all happening.

Shelley kicked and punched and shoulder-rammed at the soundless force, with no affect. Mounting her sneakered heels at the base of one of the barriers, Shelley pushed on a barrier before her, giving it all her strength, but it was like pushing on a brick wall.

She stopped pushing. Keeping both palms on the barrier, she closed her eyes. Breathed.

Calmed herself. Concentrated. She repeated Imagination a few times, eyes shut, palms on the "wall," waiting for it to disappear.

Instead, the invisible barrier pushed against her hands, moving closer, slowly, as if someone was pushing on it from the other side. Someone she could not see.

Shelley quickly placed her hands on the other three walls, all being completely still, and returning to the fourth wall, she found it still moving forward.

"No!" Shelley whimpered, both palms on the moving wall that drove her back toward the opposing wall.

Another thought breached her mind.

She turned toward the old woman who right-flanked her thirty feet away, who now had a wide open smile, displaying all her false teeth which gleamed in the midday sun, smiling as though at a circus and watching monkeys and acrobats.

"Close your eyes!!" Shelley shouted at the old woman, facing her squarely. "DON'T LOOK AT HIM!!!"

The woman continued to stare with her chilling smile, head cocked to one side.

Shelley hollered, "HELP!" a few times, hoping the caretaker would hear, but no one came. Shelley turned and placed her palms onto the moving wall once more, staring ahead. She pictured him before her – that turquoise-blue ghastly face, those abnormally shaped yellow and red eyes, his dark turquoise gloved hands pushing on the "wall."

Then Shelley attempted something she had not done before - ever.

In a soft, atone-like voice, Shelley stammered the words, "I'm s-sorry."

But it was much too late for sorries. The wall was not stopping.

There was now a foot of space in between. Shelley rested both her forearms on the moving and opposing wall, forming a W, facing away from them and toward the smiling old woman.

Her eyes still half-lidded, head slightly cocked, the woman now had a glare like that of a child whose inner forearm was being stroked while read a bedtime story."Don't look at him!"

Shelley cried.

Shelley's shoulders were now being squeezed as she continued facing the woman.

"CLOSE YOUR EYES!"

Shelley's bones began to crack, disjoint, and break, as if her body was a dry stick in a giant steel vice. Her head was squeezed like an orange in an O.J. maker, becoming a hideous purple turnip.

In a faint yet hoarse voice, the crushed woman uttered, "Close... your... eyes...."

Her head became narrower and narrower, simulating a styrofoam head slowly crushed underneath a car tire, blood streaming from her nose. Then her mouth. Then her ears. Then her eyes. Instead of the blood sticking or clinging onto the invisible force, it simply bounced off the virtual walls and fell to the grass, at their base.

Her eyes bugged out almost comically as if on springs. Brain and blood popped out from the top of her blood matted head the way sebum and water explode from a ripe pimple being squeezed.

The old woman would next get to watch the turquoise-costumed man's "rope" act ... but not until her caretaker's return.

END

Schindler's Lift

Mord McGhee

Part 1: Of testimony

"I was dead," I said. I fully understood exactly what the words meant too. I'd been choked out; snuffed, strangled, and tossed over the edge of the Earth by an honest-to-God serial killer. Since the day I opened my eyes and they arrested him, he'd been linked to more than sixty murders in New York. The High-rise Strangler, and yet, here I was … alive.

Alive and testifying against the son of a bitch.

I regarded a trimmed, respectable-looking version of the wretch who'd strangled me six months ago. Sitting calmly, in front of me. Each worriless smile fanning flames against kindling temper. As his defense attorney patted his shoulder I felt the urge to scream at those bulbous eyes, that hideous blotchy skin, those gruesome misshapen ears.

"CAN'T YOU SEE IT'S A MONSTER? KILL IT!"

Forget testifying, I should've brought the .44 Magnum I bought at a gun show two days after leaving the hospital. I would've given the old prick a round red hole through the middle of his stupid face. It was the least I could do, for what he'd done … tried to do.

Instead, my voice cracked. "The elevator," I hesitated, stumbling on the correct word the prosecutor coached me to use, "rattled." My mental notes folded neatly in a line then, "He wasn't inside. I didn't see him, I mean. It was as if he were invisible."

Judge Suttoth remained still, expression not a hair more than unnerving neutral. His gaze pierced my soul, ripping the truth back out through the wounds. We're all invisible to a man like him. Tyrant law enforcers, aliens beyond empathy. It was as close as I could get to comprehending the thoughts behind the Judge's eyes.

"I'd disliked the elevator since the first day I'd moved into that damned apartment building. It died the first time I got on," four hours I'll never get back. Four hours or six months? The elevator was nine floors of Hell. Here I was pushed to testify against the mocking smile of torment.

"Objection," the defense attorney left his seat, one hand holding a bad toupee and the other tipping an index finger at me. "Previous omens have no weight." He sat though his mouth didn't stop, "Invisible and rattled? Come on," he said. "Do you live in a comic book, Michael."

I glanced at the judge, nothing to see there. I said, "I don't, no."

"Michael, my client's life hangs on your shadowy descriptivism. Is this all you have for us?"

I heard whispers from the back of the room. "He's lying … liar… full of bullshit …" My blood ran cold. The raging temper stamped out beneath beads of sweat rolling over my cheek. I think it was perspiration. It may have been a tear.

Judge Suttoth's voice was a booming blast, "Explain to the court your meaning behind the terms in question, Mr. Densfield."

The defense attorney smirked, the turd. A minute of silence was a knuckle against gut, with force enough to bruise. I felt Judge Suttoth's hot, bourbon soaked breath puffing into the back of my head. An angry bull, prepared to gore humankind to pulp matter.

I gulped, the coaching hadn't covered explanations of the word rattle. "Sort of the sound a rattlesnake makes, I guess."

"Objection." The defense attorney frowned, "Do you have expertise in rattlesnakes, Michael?"

"No."

Judge Suttoth's seat creaked behind me. His voice a leaden funeral bell, "Continue, Mr. Densfield." I looked back in time to see arms cross. I gulped and pulled the glob of cotton away from my neck, strands stuck to the leaking scabs which refused to heal even after half a year.

I said, "Loud, unnervingly so. I considered the stairs despite a sprained ankle."

***

Part 2: Of perception

The judge's eyes performed acupuncture. I shuddered as they retracted from my flesh, slick with the juices of terror. His voice bashed the top of my skull, "Mr. Densfield, was this the first instance you became aware you weren't alone in the elevator?"

"No," I said. Dagon Heim, my would-be murderer, was behind me. Why didn't I see him? I'd asked myself a thousand times. Was the ankle hurting, distracting me? It took a deep breath and subsequent exhale before my lips quit quivering. "I never saw him."

"Allow me to rephrase the question. Was it the first time you ever saw Dagon Heim?"

My gorge rose. I wanted to leap over the bench and smash the old fish-lipped man to pieces. Rage returned high tide. I shuddered, focusing on the answer. "No. I'd seen him in a window when I came to look at the apartment. A week earlier. At least I think it was him."

The judge's chair creaked again, a brewing thunderstorm. Dagon Heim's neck folded in a grotesque way. Flabs of moist, yolky skin. His mouth opened and closed, a Piscean gasping for air through unholy gills. Or is he chewing the air?

The defense attorney said, "In the record you spoke of a flash of blue light."

"I did."

"And it was after this strange vision Dagon Heim appeared out of nowhere?"

"I don't know."

"Do you maintain your description continues to be accurate, Michael?"

"I don't know." My counsel cleared his throat, drawing the room's attention. I took the hint, clarifying. "Yes, it's accurate."

The defender's voice smoothed. "You have quite the passion," he said, "for superheroes."

"What?"

"Your adjectives are akin to the POW and BLAM in a cartoon."

"I have no idea what you're asking me."

Judge Suttoth rumbled, "Make your point, counselor."

"Flash of blue, oh, and spark." The defender stood, hands curled into fists. "Pow!"

"Spark isn't anything like pow. You're an asshole."

"Were you having a psychotic episode, Michael?"

"What?" I looked at Judge Suttoth, he'd turned to stone. I turned back, the defense attorney had stepped around the table and approached. "Screw you!"

"Your medical records indicate prior institutionalization."

"Bullsh..."

"Watch your language," stone judge bellowed, "Mr. Densfield."

"Did you lose your mind," he grinned, tapping the fold under his elbow, "or was it the drugs again?"

I wanted to rip the rug off his scalp. "I..." his beady eyes were wicked little candles, they shook me. "I was a kid. My parents checked me into rehab. It has nothing to do with him," I pointed at his client, "strangling me!"

The defense attorney turned his back and exchanged maddening smiles with my killer. "Where," he continued, "were you going on the morning in which you claim Mr. Heim was invisible, Michael?"

I had a vision of whacking the defense attorney in the head with a crow bar. "I don't know."

"We've seen your arrest history, Michael. It's part of the process vesting witnesses. We have no secrets, it's okay to talk freely. Tell us where you were going?"

"What?"

"Where were you going on March 15th, Michael? Tell us."

"How is it important?"

"Judge Suttoth decides what's important, Michael. You tell your side and he decides whether or not you're a lying, junky piece of garbage."

"Objection," my counsel perked up at last. "Mr. Densfield's past record was deemed no import. I strike as inadmissible."

"Sustained," said Judge Suttoth. "Reel it in, Mr. Insmuth."

My counsel met my gaze and mouthed the words so often coached, "Keep your mouth shut."

The defender faced me, eyes distending unnaturally. "Can we now discuss your depiction of Dagon Heim being blessed with the ability to become invisible at will?"

I gnashed my teeth. "You're twisting what I said around." A pain shot through my throat, I patted fresh droplets of blood into the cotton cloth. It had no effect curtailing his line of questioning. I hated both of them, the men standing against my testimony, more with each passing moment.

***

Part 3: Of truth

"Mr. Densfield, would you say you possess a propensity to exaggerate?"

"Look," I sighed. "What do you want from me?"

"You told police Dagon Heim was invisible. I'd like to explore this further, to set the record straight."

"We all would," Judge Suttoth clapped thunder.

"You said invisible. Either you didn't notice my client or he had a way of turning invisible. Which is it? The two are very different things."

"Invisible's a figure of speech. I didn't…"

"Rubbish. I think you were high on dope and looking for more the morning in question. Weren't you, Michael?"

"I hate your guts." I was on my feet, unsure of how I got there.

Judge Suttoth slapped a gavel against the bench. BAM-BAM. "Calm down, Mr. Densfield, answer the question." I glanced at Judge Suttoth. My heart sank. True neutral.

"Maybe I chose the wrong word."

The defender turned to the judge, "Your Honor, I move to strike Michael Densfield's testimony."

"Denied. Are you through, counselor?"

"Judge Suttoth, this man is a heroin addict."

Whispers from the back … "Suck a cock … man-whore … anything for a fix."

I leapt to my feet, shaking angrily. "Fuc…"

Judge Suttoth cut the crap, electric blast of volume. "Motion denied. Lighten up, Mr. Insmuth."

The defender pointed at Judge Suttoth, "If an American taxpayer is executed by an Israeli firing squad, it's on you."

Judge Suttoth blinked. The paint on the wall melted behind him. His voice narrowed into a single cannon's fire, "Do not raise your finger at me, son."

Color drained from the defender's cheeks. "I apologize, your Honor."

"This once," the judge snarled, "I accept your apology. This once…"

The defender gulped. He turned towards me with slow, deliberate steps. "Am I to understand correctly that you chose my client," he said, "Dagon Heim, out of a police line-up."

"I did."

"So he wasn't entirely invisible? Mostly see-through, perhaps?"

"He wasn't invisible, he was unassuming."

"And yet, you selected Mr. Heim out of a line-up."

"I… uh…"

"You're a very confused man."

"I…"

"With quite a history of drug addiction." He paused, lashing further into his line of reasoning. "Do you always turn your back to strangers, Michael?"

"What?"

"You got on the elevator in front of an unassuming man and turned your back to him."

"Who faces people on an elevator?"

The defense attorney closed the gap between us, slamming his fist against the wooden bench. "You picked Dagon Heim out of a police line because you'd seen him many times before. You've been stalking him, in fact. That's the whole truth of it, isn't it?"

***

Part 4: Of symptoms

My brave prosecutor scratched with pen on a notepad and I caught his eye. He held it up, it read: STRANGLE. I nodded and leveled a finger at the blue-gray old man across the room, "He slipped a rag around my neck and strangled me. I died in the elevator."

The defense attorney offered a toothy grin, "And yet, here you are, Michael."

I heard whispers from the back rise again. "Drug addict ... needle in flesh ... withdrawal."

I looked for the source, the seats were empty except for one woman. She held fabric in a ball over her face and rocked side to side. Her garb looked old, from the forties or fifties. Red dress, red hat with a wide brim. She seemed familiar, somehow. Yet not.

"Nobody can tell me why I woke up," I said. "I was definitely dead."

The defender made an elaborate gesture. He was a hand-talker, something else to hate about him. "It's of my opinion you chose Dagon Heim out of the line-up because you're a vengeful Jew and he's a German who got out before the end of the war."

"What're you talking about? I'm not a Jew. I have no clue what he is, nor do I care."

"You hate Germans, one and all. Like me, right Michael?"

The whispers rose to crescendo. "Hate crime ... poor old man ... filthy hippie."

"Who keeps whispering? I am not!"

Judge Suttoth severed the floor with one snap of tongue, "Enough."

I swallowed and looked around. The woman in red was gone. My mind went places it had no business going. When I turned back, Judge Suttoth said, "It's time to read your prepared statement, Mr. Densfield."

The defender approached Judge Suttoth, hands against hip. "Hypoxia," he said.

The judge remained still.

"A heroin overdose which produces suppression of oxygen to the brain. Also causes lingering psychosis, your Honor."

I shook my head, "I never overdosed."

Whispers from out of nowhere: "Junky creep ... scumbag ... wait until his mother hears."

"His addiction makes him prone to hallucinations, your Honor. It's why he didn't see Dagon Heim the day in question. There were no lights, no sparks, no invisible men. There was only a drug addict going through some sickening stage of Hypoxia, on his way out the door desperate to score another syringe." The defender wasn't done. I saw something in his eyes which wasn't there before. Infinity, black holes of deep space ... swallowing universes whole and spitting out bits of planetary bone. I pulled back, shoving the chair against the wall. His voice grew stranger, brash and distorted. It was as though he spoke through a megaphone. "Dagon Heim wasn't there at all, was he Michael? You picked him out of a line-up because you hate the German people." His index finger became a battering ram, swinging back and forth into my heart with each word. "You imagine they're all Nazi bastards because of your own, inbred prejudices."

"No!" dabbing spots of blood with cotton.

"Admit it, Michael. An elderly German man smiles at you every day, living in the same building you live in, and it grinds into your brain because of all the suffering his kind is responsible for meting out."

"No!"

The judge's voice splashed cold water between us, "Sit down, both of you."

The defender growled, "Godwin's Law."

I drew breath, unable to speak. Outrage dragged me to the floor as Judge Suttoth slammed his gavel. BAM-BAM-BAM. "Sit down, Mr. Insmuth, or I'll have you removed from my court."

"Tell them, Densfield," the defender's eyes wild. "Tell them you were stoned out of your fucking mind and you're a no-good sack of shit! Tell them." Our faces closed, mere inches apart. I felt his breath, he undoubtedly felt mine. The gavel slammed until the world began to spin.

I closed my eyes. Paper rustled, doors banged, murmurs passed, and the public defender laughed.

Damned whispers: "He's cracking... worthless liar... don't trust the junky."

***

Part 5: Of violence

I didn't care for the way I shook as I recounted the past.

"I stepped inside, the floor... uh, shifted. I remember thinking I should take the stairs so I didn't get stuck in the elevator again. But my ankle was bad. I didn't see anyone else in the car, invisible or not."

"Understood," Judge Suttoth nodded. "Proceed."

"The light flickered as the door closed. I think I saw blue sparks through the cracks between the floor and the hallway," the defense attorney scoffed, I ignored him. "I watched the numbers drop from nine, but I don't remember when he attacked. Six, maybe." I paused and dabbed my neck, the spots deep crimson as I pulled cotton away.

Judge Suttoth said, "Take your time, Michael." The boom of volume replaced by deep timber.

"Sorry," my breath quickened, pain ripping through my body. I need a break. I need a fix. I said, "He latched onto me from behind. Steel coil strong. I had no chance, he'd done this before. The next thing I knew my eyes popped out of their sockets, my world turned dark red. It was fast, I would've screamed if I could've. There wasn't time to do anything but die. The crush he put on, it was unbreakable. My cheek hit ground and the only thing I could see was the writing on the wall."

"The writing on the wall?" Jude Suttoth said. "As in you died?"

"No. Real words on the wall. Schindler Elevator Company, 1928."

Judge Suttoth looked at me in a curious way. Confusion? Pity? I couldn't be sure. His gaze passed to the defender and he said, "Three days later Mr. Densfield awakened from death. Anything further, counselor?"

"No, your Honor."

***

Part 6: Of death

52

While I was dead I her, an angel. Her face had been indescribably beautiful. It won't even appear in my memory any longer and I'm glad for it. I'd fallen in love instantly and wouldn't be able to let her go. Those gleaming golden robes, her skin as pure as freshly driven snow. She smelled of vanilla and sandalwood. Everything about her perfect, except the bloodied sword dripping crimson droplets onto my bare toes. Our eyes met and her wings exploded into flames, she curled her finger with a seductive smile. Beckoning me forth, to go with her. The doctors told me illusions were brain starving for oxygen. I don't believe them, she was real. Time evaporated; a week, a month...

It was four months before they sent me from the hospital. "If you continue to experience visions," they said, "call us."

The extended BEEEEEEEEEEEEEEEEEP woke me up. My heart monitor stopped, nobody came to help. It's then the creatures without faces came. Featureless phantoms, swirling around me. Where they brushed my naked skin it felt ice cold. I couldn't scream as they began to tear me apart. Their laughter taunts me to this day. One clear voice rose above the rest, "He'll beg for death when it comes at last. The master has marked his soul."

In and out; cringing.

A rush of motion, lights, and tingling euphoria. I felt my fingers curl of their own accord, I wasn't making the shots. The spot in my arm reserved for past escapism burned in one tight spot, as though a lit cigarette had been thrusted into the skin.

In and out; recoiling.

A woman in blue pulled my shirt to the side, fiddling with a tube jutting out from a nipple. She pinched and chuckled, "Mmm, mmm. That's gonna smart, boy." She tweaked and tapped buttons of pain I'd never known before.

In and out; hyperventilating.

The glint of metal was all I could see, shining... reflecting something as yellow and hot as the sun. It was one of the faceless specters, I felt nothing though the tip of the blade sank beneath flesh, splitting a red line from belly button to shoulder. I couldn't scream, I couldn't breathe. I could only shudder as streams of blood crept through the forest of chest hair.

In and out; screaming.

Shimmering blue nails peeled me apart as though opening a tent flap. There lay the juicy red and black innards I'd spent a lifetime keeping inside. They wiggled and squirmed, carrion worms devouring me from within. A hump formed, up and down... pushing out from the distended, squiggling ropes of my intestinal slime. My brain let loose of its hold on sanity wholesale, without leaving marks where the finger nails separated.

In and out; what lies beyond.

All stop.

I was alone, intact.

I'd gotten wet somehow. It was another mystery I accepted without question because my legs were tired from treading water. I lay back, swimming the dead man's float through a what could only be an ocean, as it went on further than my eyes could see. This vision of limitless sea was the sole direction in which I could travel. Bobbing up and down, lungs soaking up salt water and slime.

I hit something, thick and heavy. I screamed at first though stopped both because my throat was on fire and because I realized it was land, nothing more. This was no conventional surf, this was a pasty dark cobweb dotted with spots of greasy black grass and jagged barbed rocks. The marine noise and blurry sense were all I had left.

In and out; direction.

I felt for something to prove I was not in a dream state, using hands, elbows, knees... until I decided the floor was solid. The hair on the back of my neck reared on end. I peered over my shoulder, afraid monsters pursued.

Menacing gaze heat.

However, behind there was not but vast, endless black water. I lay before a sprawling landscape, filled with outlandish shades. Crooked things, bent and angry.

In and out; time.

Madness slipped over me like a coat on a cold winter's night. The air itself thick with vile sludge. My bare feet slapped down again and again, breaking spent syringes. I screamed, averting my gaze. When I screwed courage enough to face the horror I saw glass and human wreckage. Bones bleached gray, every step more skeletons. A decomposing head with swollen, round eyes contemplated my reason for intruding its slumber. I kicked it, laughing, "Alas, poor Yorick!"

As I followed its trail over the sun-stained bones I saw a jutting structure. Distant, yet calling me. I approached, it grew steadily as I stumbled ahead. Its walls were thick, matted fibrous thorn briar. The jagged teeth nipped at me, hungrily. I pulled a hand back, bleeding. The trail opened, thorn briars receding into drab clay walls. My hand left a bloody print and I pulled closer to what I perceived as being safety within shelter. I followed the monolith's angles, up, up into the sky. "How?" I gasped, gathering a new understanding. The entire face was covered with bloody handprints.

I threw my back against cool clay.

These red and brown marks weren't random testaments of passage. No, this was a grisly scene. Art wrought from the bowels of the abyss. Men kneeling before a spider a hundred times its worshipper's size. There at its spiny legs the kneeling men placed rocks.

"No, not rocks... heads!"

I whirled to run but stumbled, finding I'd dropped deeper into darkness surrounding the monolith. Another piece of abhorrent graffiti came into view. Men on boats, killing whales with spear guns. "Not whales... what are they?" Before I could discern, a third carving caught my eye. It had been scrawled in wild, jagged slashes and She was terrible to behold.

A head full of snakes, round swelling breasts, a maw full of great white shark teeth. "Medusa," I hissed. "No... more. Worse!" My words became cries, my cries became bloodcurdling screams. I was aware I'd gone... mad.

The shadows came alive. Narrow headed figures with small, loathsome fingers crushing against my windpipe. Among the jet black writhing, I saw armbands... bearing Nazi swastikas. A voice tore a cavern through my brain. It spoke one word, over and again. A pulsating, slavering chant, "Balakot. Balakot. Balakot." The dark came for me, with a thousand eyes.

I'll never know how I escaped, if, in fact, I had.

***

Part 7: Of torment

My eyes adjusted to vivid brightness. I was in a hospital bed; that much was clear. That, and there before me was Dagon Heim. Sunlight spilled through an open window and it cast deep black curves over his face. He came at me, cloth snapping in hand. I opened my mouth to yell but no sound came.

He howled terrifying laughter. Hopelessness gorged upon my being, reality spinning out of control. I heard the unmistakable sound of torture... wailing cries accompanied by thumping voodoo drums.

BEEP. BEEP. BEEP. BEEP.

55

I gasped, a bead of sweat crawled down the left side of my breast, a skittering liquid centipede. It hung from my ribcage until it fell, splashing into...

...splashing into all things happening.

The dream dissolved. I sat alone in the corridor outside Judge Suttoth's courtroom. A wave of nausea locked mortal cobra combat with an inner mongoose. My gaze was drawn to the blurry glass facing the outside world. Something moved there, among a line of brown and green. The blur comes into focus.

Trees. A hanged corpse rocking in the breeze, branch above worn with rope-cut notches.

I do not know her face, it's bent and twisted under pain of a broken neck. Her eyes are open, pale and milky white. Streaks of grey curse her head beneath a red hat. The dress adorning her body is stained with the dirt of passing time. Entrails drip from beneath, turning the white slip into a brownish-black border between dress and ankle. A thin line of crimson streaks towards her chipped toenails and broken toes.

I edge towards the glass, unable to cease staring

The hangman's rope ends with a black, red, and white fabric...

...a Nazi flag.

The sky melts, dripping waxen clouds over a buttery moon. I heard his breath first, and I knew Dagon Heim was back. I shuddered, footsteps coming quickly. The muscles beneath my bandage pulsated, dreadful memory of the strangler's tool. I died in that lift...

...and I cheated death by the grace of God.

Cannot breathe... cannot breathe!

I'd walked over the back of a spider the size of the moon.

Its eyes...its eyes!

I'd overdosed on heroin.

The needle... the needle!

I'd seen that which should not be.

The Stranglers... the Stranglers!

Dagon Heim pressed his Hellish garrote, covering my eyes. "Shhh," he promised the end would be swift. A split second later, the blindfold lifted. I was back in Judge Suttoth's courtroom.

Alive ... alive!

***

"State your name," Judge Suttoth resounded.

"Dagon Heim." The German accent subtle, though there nonetheless.

The bailiff held the Bible. I noticed Dagon Heim avoided touching it. "Do you swear to tell the truth, so help you God?"

"I affirm to tell the truth, though you will not wish to hear it once I've begun."

Judge Suttoth sat stoic. The defense attorney approached, "May I, your Honor?"

"This is an inquest, counselor. Save the theatrics for trial."

"Understood, your Honor." He turned to his client, "Tell us who you are, Dagon."

"People call me Dag." Dagon Heim smiled, sweet as pie. "I am the second son of a police man named Yuri Garter Heim. My mother's name was Anna Böse. I was born in Bad Radkersburg, Austria-Hungary. My brother was the Nazi criminal known as Doctor Death, Aribert Heim."

"Thank you, Dag." The public defender nodded, "Do you understand why you're here today?"

The old man's crooked finger pointed at me. "I am accused of killing him, though he is not dead."

Ghostly whispers: Alive... he lies... should die!

I covered my ears with palms. The courtroom blended into shapes both light and dark, twisting together morbid tones into sneering skulls.

In and out; trip.

I heard my brother's voice. "It's not your fault, Mikey. Hang in there. It's almost over." The sting of a needle bit into soft flesh opposite my elbow. Black, inky ooze devoured existence, leaving me naked under plumes of rising smoke. I saw a gate with a sign, a chimney reaching for sky. A decorated sign above the gate read 'Belzec' and though I didn't know it then, I had opened my eyes in the midst of a death camp.

Ashes pumping darkness overhead whispered, "Come closer..."

One by one, smoky pillars assembled into a charcoal-colored mass. It mutated into an old man with fish-lips, bulbous eyes, stretching a wrap of cloth towards me... towards my unprotected throat. I screamed until he locked the cloth, my neck bones popped. He howled as thunder struck, "I am eternal! I am Todesengel! I am the Angel of Death!" I smelled the sour, metallic reek of blood. A bead of his sweaty filth fell into my gasping mouth. Silver moonlight painted streaks through my field of vision...

...I opened my eyes, the night terror had receded once more.

I lifted my head. "A pillow?" I gasped, clutching the throbbing skin below my chin. I was lying in a cot within my father's cabin near Lake Wallenpaupack. A featureless silhouette lurked in the hoary glow and though I screamed his name, it wasn't Dagon Heim.

It had my brother's voice, "Balakot's children are coming for you."

"What?"

"The Stranglers, we have always been and will always be. From cave to grave, merciful and swift to those who are not."

I thrust off the bed shouting. The silhouette crawled to an open window and jumped. I was on fire with a passion to end this. I followed, scrambling forward as grunts of anger and pain left frothed lips. My legs betrayed me, I fell face down. My father stepped out, offering a hand to help me up. "Keep your eye on the ball, son," he said. "You'll get through this."

In and out; the promise.

Whispers: "The sons of a stranglers born of the grandsons of a stranglers, whose father strangled before them."

I gagged on vomit, couldn't stop. The words as steel spikes spearing my cranium. "NO!" I cried out. No matter how hard I squeezed my head, the whispering voices wouldn't go away.

We are eternal, sons of the dark. We are coming for you."

My father's hand pressed against my cheek. Rough, familiar touch. "Don't listen to the voices, Mikey. They're not there. It's the drug." Agony peeled me apart until I felt his steady hand on my shoulder. I smelled the cologne he kept on his dresser when we were kids. My father's voice anchored the last wisps of life in me, which would've made perfect sense if he hadn't died when I was seventeen. "We love you. We're here for you, son. Never give up."

The End
The Beginning

The Great Satyr

Jeremy Ferretti

I don't know when I began thinking the thought, 'I don't know where I am or how I got here.', but at some point I realized I'd been repeating it over and over.

The night was a humid hell. In the middle of dark woods at night. I was staring at a tree stump. In the dead, lifeless block of wood was embedded an axe. Old and worn, but no rust or dirt. It had been used recently.

My head was throbbing. I touched it to find my head was bleeding.

I could tell by the hollow pain in my throat and lungs I had been running long and hard. Something had been chasing me, but by what?

Then there was something ... I could remember a woman sobbing in terror. Was that woman me?

There were no crickets chirping. I remembered hearing crickets before. I remember hearing them when I was listening for something, but they had stopped now. Why had they stopped?

All at once, the birds hiding in the trees took flight, creating a flickering, amorphous black blob that danced against the pale grey of the moonlit clouds. Something spooked the birds and it was coming my way.

I knew you're not supposed to exert yourself after a head injury, but I decided to make the exception when I knew I was being chased by ... something.

I ran through the woods, in the opposite direction of where the birds flew from. I couldn't remember what I was running from, only how it made me feel. A dark, sick pit in my stomach, of tumor of despair with a mouth that whispered the doubt that I might not actually make it out of here ... or even worse, I might make it out with scars worse than death.

My head throbbed and I started to dizzy. *Christ?* I wondered. *How bad was this head injury?* Forget the thing stalking me, what if I didn't recover from the head wound?

My foot caught on upturned roots and I hit the ground. The spinning in my head. I felt like I was drowning in dirt. There was no remorse any more, no feelings. Just a horrible confusion as my brain tried to stand ... tried to balance itself, but my equilibrium was so completely messed up.

My spinning view caught on the side of a tree and I focused on the misplaced color on it. The spinning slowed ... until finally it almost stopped. The vertigo was then replaced by that sick feeling in the pit of my stomach.

The side of the tree had been scored, the way a bear would mark its territory ... but these weren't bear claws. This was something completely different. They were definitely claws of some kind, but they were sharp and cut deep. Almost as if it were done by heavy razor wire being whipped hard into the tree.

I re-assessed my surroundings and could've sworn I saw a faint orange light in the distance. Fire? I thought.

I jogged lightly towards the light, it was too dark to watch my footing at full sprint and I couldn't risk shaking my head up again. Another fall like that and I would slow myself down faster than I could get by sprinting. If there was a camp fire, there must be campers. They would know where we were and where to go.

There was a camp fire, but no campers. No tents or bags, the only sign of life being a few broken branches and crumpled leaves.

Something flickered off the camp fire light, under some brush. Something shiny had fallen into the brush. I looked closer and saw it was a locket or a medallion of some sort. I couldn't reach it; it was deep in the brush. I got down on my belly and reached into the thick, thorny brush, cutting up the sleeves and shoulders of the shirt I was wearing. It was just out of reach.

BOOM! BOOM! BOOM!

The sounds of a heavy animal barreled towards me and I panicked. I tried to pull my arm out of the brush, but only got it more deeply tangled in the thorns. I managed to turn around to see a silhouette against the campfire.

The thing towered over my helpless, trapped body, roughly two times my height and width. It was covered in light, fauna-like hair, but it's rippling, twitching, sinewy muscles were visible beneath. Its feet were hooves that could crush bones, with two legs bent backward in an extra joint that goats have. The torso was that of a man, although hunched over, it was still massively tall. Its face was obscured by the darkness but I could make out the vague goat-like shape of its head complete with demonic, twirling horns.

Unlike a demon, there was no malevolent intelligence behind this creature. It seemed to be a lumbering hate-beast. From six feet away, I could smell its breath, that of a landfill flowing down over me.

It raised the blunt object it carried in its left hand and clubbed me on the other side of the head with it, knocking me out.

***

"It just won't stop. It can't stop. I don't think the world will let it stop. You don't understand how it's built, Nikki. The thing is a goddamn monster! And that doesn't even begin to describe it. I don't think there are any words that can describe the thing. It can be anywhere and everywhere at once. It's not smart, but it always seems to be cutting you off, predicting when you'll do something or just waiting for the worst time to hurt you again."

In the span of one monologue, Diana McBride went from the appearance of a normal person you pass on the street to a sniveling wretch of a person. She was a shell of the woman I once knew. It was hard to look at this woman with anything but extreme pity. It was the kind of pity you give that twisted hobo with ten pounds of snot plastered to his beard who sits on the subway floor clutching the pole begging for his mother.

"Diana, you need to stop this."

She turned her glance upward. She was lying on the floor, unable to pick herself up. "Stop what?"

"This sad, self-pity crying crap. It's not going to help; it's only going to make things worse." I almost punched myself in the face, immediately regretting the words coming out of my mouth. "Try to pull yourself together."

Diana started trembling. She wanted to be angry, but all the fight had left this woman long ago. Instead of anger coming, a shaking fear was triggered. "H-how can you say something like that?"

I had made the conscious decision to start to work on my compassion, but the words always came out wrong. "I'm sorry. I'm not good with ... helping people. It's not my forte."

To my surprise, her weak trembles managed to turn into something fierce for only a moment. "Your forte is taking care of these types of things!" she shrieked.

"No, it's not," I said. "I merely report on these things. I don't intentionally solve problems, I observe them."

"What about that kid you used to date, Zack? Zeke? You helped him!"

"I didn't have a choice."

"That's not true, Nikki! This thing broke my knees and forced me to watch as it ripped my husband to pieces!"

I cringed, knowing the rest of the story.

The anger started to disappear once again. "And all you did was write an article about it and call it a day." Her nose was getting blocked up from the sobbing. "And then when I thought it was over, when I could walk again ... it came back." She looked up at me like a starving child begging for leftovers. "It came back."

I couldn't make eye contact with her. I remembered the pictures of the crime scene. It turned my stomach worse than anything had in recent memory.

***

"It's all a deep end."

Through a blur I could see I was in a concrete basement of some sort. I was back in the woods. Well, in the basement of a cabin in the woods. The blow from the creature had jogged my memory. I was investigating this thing as a favor to Diana. Was I supposed to be hunting it? Why hadn't I any weapons? Why had I gone alone? What was I thinking?

"It's all a deep end," a voice repeated.

"Who is that?" I asked. The basement was dark, the only light coming from the small window at the top of the wall. "Who?"

"Thomas," the voice answered.

I tried to stand up to find my wrists were shackled and chained to the ground. I tugged hard on the chains. There was no escape from this mess.

"Thomas, do you have any idea what is going on?" I asked.

"I-I try to. It's hard. It's ..." there was a very long pause as the voice searched for the right word to say "... hard."

"What's hard? What's wrong?"

"He hit me hard last time. I don't ..." another pause. "... remember."

The moon shone through the clouds and throughout the basement window for a moment, giving me a view of Thomas as he sat against the wall. His eyes were vacant, his hair was completely soaked with blood. It looked deformed in a way, as if the skull had been broken. White fluid was leaking out of his nose like a faucet. I could see he was trying to say something but nothing was coming out. Then the clouds covered up what I could see.

"Christ ..."

"Too much work. I'm sleeping."

"No! Thomas, don't go to sleep. Not now!"

Ignoring my pleas, I heard Tom shuffle into a laying down position until the sound of shuffling ceased and the sound of loud mouth breathing started.

"Tom, wake up." I wasn't getting through to him.

Oh God what am I going to do? I've been through worse. I can handle this. What's the procedure? What do you have on you? You can reach your pockets, check them.

I found a lighter in my back pocket and used it to illuminate the basement. The basement was mostly empty except for a couple of pieces of randomly assorted rusted metal and the occasional human bone.

The room was supposed to be a stone grey color, but it had been painted a new color. A dark brown that my eyes could recognize as dried blood. I was chained to the ground by a huge lock. The thing was apparently smart enough to know how to use a key. Or maybe it would just break my arms off getting me out.

I shone the lighter over Thomas, asleep in the fetal position, his hands curled against his belly. He seemed to be in his middle age and his injuries looked worse than I thought. In addition to the visibly deformed skull, I could see bleached bone poking out through his shin. Then I noticed the man wasn't chained down. He wasn't being restrained by anything expect maybe his own injuries.

He was out of my reach, but I managed, by stretching, to nudge him with my foot. It took a couple of kicks before he woke up, scared. He sat up straight and moaned, pulling his head back. He was holding something large and grey in his hands. A key. The bastard was holding the key to my chains the entire time. The creature wasn't smart enough to lock me up, but this bastard still had the intelligence left to do it.

For just a moment I became furious, then I really looked at what was going on. I couldn't blame this man. The amount of physical damage this man suffered to his brain was probably incomparable to the psychological damage this monster inflicted.

I had my suspicions before, but this creature was no ordinary physical entity, it was something else. It had some sort of deep, evil presence. It was something between worlds. Something that shouldn't be seen, but was something that shouldn't interact but did.

Thomas woke and started wailing. Staring straight up at the ceiling wailing like a dying animal. I felt like my emotions were dying, seeing something that sad, but the pity and sadness was immediately turned to terror when I heard the response of the Satyr: a distant but trumpeting bellow coming far from outside.

Thomas' wailing immediately ceased and he fell completely still.

"Thomas," I said. "Tom." No response. "David!" I yelled. He looked towards me, finally being pulled from the trance. "Dave, you're going to need to give me that key. I can get us out of this, but only if you give me that key." He didn't understand any of it.

I motioned with two hands to come closer. He didn't. I tried communicating with puppy dog eyes, and clasped my hands together, hoping to convey the idea of "please" to him.

He dragged himself towards me to get a better look at me. I nodded in approval and smiled as best as I could.

When he was within arm's reach I snatched the key from him, he retreated back to his corner in fright. I went to unlocking myself. I could hear the creature's heavy hooves closing in on the cabin and I started to shake. I couldn't get the key into the hole. The hooves falling on the earth got heavier.

The front door of the cabin slammed open and I heard the hooves breaking some of the floorboards as the thing stomped towards the cellar door.

David was now convulsing in fear in the corner. I had unlocked myself but the thing had already opened the door. Thinking quick, put my unlocked wrists to the side, hiding them from view and slumped against the wall, pretending to be unconscious.

The Satyr stomped down the concrete steps. The man was now in a full fledged panic, moaning and begging the creature for protection or respite or forgiveness. I cracked my eyes open just a little bit.

I could barely see, my only sight illuminated by the bit of moonlight coming through the small window.

The creature was bearing down on the man, moving its face closer to his, breathing a misty hot breath that I could smell from the other side of the room. I shuddered, smelling the garbage breath. The creature turned to me in an instant.

My eyes closed on reaction and I tried my best to remain still. The creature was facing me, but it wasn't moving. I could tell by the pungency of its breath; it was standing still watching me intently, seeing if I moved.

"I'm sorry," the man muttered.

The creature turned back to the man, aggressively. I cracked my eyes and saw the man holding out empty hands. The hateful tension built as the creature moved its face closer to the man's. He tried opening his mouth.

In a blind fury, the Satyr started swinging its balled fists into the man's head. It wasn't hitting with all of its strength, it was as if the thing was toying with him. But there was no doubt, it was planning to break its toy. Blood splattered across the room and got on my face as the thing brought one of its fists down on top of his head. The man howled in pain.

The Satyr bellowed a hateful, intimidating roar in the dying man's face. I used the opportunity to shuffle myself towards the stairs.

Finally, with one massive swing across the man's cheek, the man fell to the ground, immobile, blood seeping from every hole in his head along with the new ones put there by the creature.

The creature became infuriated and started beating the dead man and kicking it across the room. It swung its massive hoof into the dead man's belly and sent it into the corner of the room where I was previously chained up. The body slid across the ground and dragged the chains across the floor.

The creature paused, realizing I was no longer in the same corner and turned to see me at the foot of the stairs. It roared and barreled towards me with incredible speed. I reached down and grabbed at whatever I could. I picked up a piece of what seemed to be rusted metal and swung at the creature. By pure luck, it was a sharp piece, and I managed to put a huge slash in the creature's belly. The Satyr fell backward.

I ran up the stairs, gripping the rusty piece of jagged metal and never looked back. Pure instinct took over and adrenaline ran through me.

The cabin had been out of commission for an extremely long time, nothing traces of humanity remained in it. I spent no time taking any of the details in and burst through the front doors, running for my life.

***

"I'm sorry Nikki, don't do it. If you see it, you're cursed for life. There's no escaping it. It will find you," Diana said over the phone.

"I'll deal with it." I had reached the woods ten minutes ago and was trying psych myself up. The disparaging call from Diana didn't help.

"Nikki, I'm sorry for coming to you. You don't have to do this," she said.

"I know, but I'm going to anyway. I always do."

"It's not worth it."

I hung up the phone and looked through my bag. It was packed with everything I could possibly need for any paranormal encounter; a gun with silver bullets, white sage, a stake, holy water, a cattle prod, mace. I picked the pistol up and regretted not bringing something bigger.

"Fuck it," I said to myself and left my car parked at the edge of the road. "Whatever's in here won't survive six bullets to the face."

***

The adrenaline was jumpstarting my memories, the forest was starting seem familiar. I remembered passing the cabin earlier, when it was dusk out. I could still make it out of here, even with the beast behind me. Whatever damage it had done to my brain was not permanent; I could still make it out.

I ran at a half sprint, picking my legs up high, making sure I wouldn't catch my legs on any upturned roots or branches. Far behind me, I heard the sound of the cabin door cracking off its hinges and flying into the night. I tried to ignore the sound and focus only on what was directly in front of me, but the beat of the monsters hooves on the earth was too loud and imposing to ignore.

It was gaining on me faster and faster. Even at my most desperate, adrenaline-induced best, I knew I couldn't outrun it. I lost control and began to weep openly. It could run at least two times faster than me and showed no signs of slowing down. I, on the other hand was already on my last few breaths, I was completely worn out, exhausted, and I could barely breathe. The entire thing was hopeless.

I stopped, fell to my knees and put my face down in the dead leaves, accepting my fate. When I stopped, so did the creature. I looked behind me, expecting to see it staring in the distance, but saw nothing. As I scanned the dark forest for any sign of it, the putrid landfill smell filled my nostrils.

The creature was two steps away from me, bearing down with hateful, animal eyes.

It should've taken it at least half a minute to catch up with me, but there it was, right in front of me. There was no questioning it, the thing defied any form of reason or logic. Somehow, although powered by dumb, bestial intellect, it could manipulate this forest with its own will.

The creature moved closer, breathing directly into my face, making me almost wretch. I reacted by plunging the rusty piece of jagged metal deep between its ribs. It howled in pain and surprise, making flocks of birds fly away.

Still horrified that it might still live through the stabbing, I ran up to it and kicked my boot into the jagged metal, pushing it deeper into the Satyr's flesh. In no less than a second, the thing dematerialized into a cloud of mist vaguely representing a human form. The jagged piece of metal fell to the ground.

I observed the cloud of mist, which was now falling apart in the light wind and picked up the piece of metal. It had no blood on it.

I sighed, assuming I had hallucinated the entire thing. Then, as if the mist was suddenly being sucked inside of a vacuum, turned into a canonical shape and entered into my mouth and nose. The horrid burning hair and garbage smell entered my reality once again and I collapsed, my joints all locking up.

The entirety of my body was in pain, and there was nothing I could do. MY muscles burned, my bones ached. I had zero control. My back arched and my arms and legs flexed in. Then it all stopped.

I grabbed the jagged piece of metal and started stabbing myself wildly in the wrist. My mouth started to yell, "YOU FUCKING DUMB, JUNKIE WHORE!"

It was as if all of my self-hate was dialed up to 11 and going higher. "FUCKING PIECE OF SHIT!" I began to stab the rusty metal deeper into my arm. "PAIN ISN'T ENOUGH FOR YOU!"

My mind was melted and there was nothing left but a blackened blob of curdled hate. I deserved this, I told myself. I need this! It's the only thing someone like me is apt for. I can sit around an judge but when it comes down to it, I'm the fucking filth of the world. I'm a failure, a waste of air.

I put the metal deep into my arm and started to twist and dig around into my wrist until I couldn't conduct my left pinky anymore.

"FUCKING END IT, JUNKIE BITCH!" I took the piece of metal, shaking and pushed it into the side of my neck, intending to saw it across my neck.

I had a single moment of clarity. This was the Satyr's last ditch effort to kill me. This voice wasn't mine, it was his.

Although the dial was still turned to 11, I managed to put the jagged metal down and observe what I had done to myself. The wound in my wrist as a mangled mess and part of my hand was no longer moving. I vomited. It was putrid, the smell of garbage and burnt hair.

I picked myself up and walked, exhausted, a few miles to my parked car. The sun was rising now and the sky was a light, but dim, blue. I would've cried tears of joy upon finding my beat up green Volkswagen, but I was too low on fluids to do anything but collapse against the side of the car, mouth a gait. I sat there for somewhere around ten minutes, catching my breath, not knowing if I'd be able to pick myself up.

I stood up and locked myself in my car when I heard the thumping again. The same thumping of hooves on forest earth. I started the car and sped down the highway, on a beeline back to New York City.

The beat of the hooves never stopped, I could hear it in my head. It's been six months and I swear I can still hear those hooves on the pavement outside my door.

The Dark Net

Jeff C. Stevenson

"You can't take death so personally," Dr. Baxter said. "It's not like it has a particular vendetta against you or the ones you love. We're all going to die."

"Really?" Jacob said. "After what I've told you, you still don't think that I've had much more than my share of death? Much, much more than anyone you've known?"

***

Death first manifested Itself in all Its dark glory when Jacob was only ten. It wiped the planet clean of his parents and younger sister in a swift and fiery car crash. To make it all the more horrific, the teenage drunk driver survived with no injuries. His parents said it was a miracle their son had survived.

Jacob moved to another state to live with his father's parents, his only relatives, but they were already in their eighties and within five months, they too passed away. His grandfather was struck dumb with a stroke a month after Jacob arrived, and he died a week later. Jacob's grandmother had already begun fading away into the soft, smothering fabric of dementia and was sent to a care facility the first day of spring and was dead before July 4. The courts placed Jacob with a foster family. Since they were not blood relatives, no harm came to them. After he moved out to attend college, they quickly lost contact with him.

When he was twenty-three, he met and fell helplessly in love with Danielle. She was a single mother and they planned to marry and he would adopt her beautiful daughter, Rachel. But during the wedding reception, a fire started in the kitchen and the ceiling vents sucked up the smoke and flames. The support beams collapsed, blocking the front entrance. Seven people died in the fire, including Danielle and Rachel.

From that moment on, Jacob took Death personally, knew that a bond had formed between them. They were on a first-name basis, and like a deadly shadow, It clung to his thoughts and buried Itself deep into his mind and made a snug home for Itself. Jacob returned the devotion, making it his one passion to somehow outwit It, to somehow jump over Its yawning chasm and Its impossibly long reach. Each time he read about a death in the paper or heard about one online or on TV, he took it personally, as if Death was simply reminding him that every day, He would take someone no matter how much grief it caused or how much it would destroy and uproot the lives of those involved.

Death had made Jacob a loner from an early age, a sober-minded child with a wary and untrusting view of life. As he aged, Jacob learned that whatever kept you safe or loved or secure could be taken from you as quickly as changing the channel on the TV. After the death of Danielle and Rachel, he focused all his energy and thoughts on Death, Its nature, Its origin, and the possibility of defeating It.

Jacob knew how many people It consumed each day (more than 153,000), each year (56 million), and by what method (cardiovascular disease for most, followed by cancer, diabetes and then lung diseases). He didn't think the obsession was morbid, it was simply a matter of gathering intelligence about a cruel and relentless enemy that had invaded his life when he was a child and never planned to leave.

He knew Death could lunge at him at any moment; a car crash or freak accident or being in the wrong place at the wrong time, something that would render him dead, something he would never see coming. A surprise attack, events he couldn't control and had no say in their set up or outcome. Because most of the tactics Death used were health related, Jacob kept himself fit and healthy and ate a well-balanced diet. If at all possible, he didn't want to die of a natural death or by his body betraying him and shutting itself down one day.

He didn't think his fixation was out of the ordinary or that he was mentally ill. The mystery and secrets of Death were top of mind for anyone who had ever stopped to think about the meaning of their life and their purpose on the planet. Everyone was curious about what—if anything—happened beyond the veil, what awaited him or her once the moral coil was shed.

For years he had discussed the topic with his physician and as always, had been disappointed when Dr. Baxter had once again dismissively said, "You can't take death so personally. It's not like it has a particular vendetta against you or the ones you love. We're all going to die."

Jacob thought differently.

He obtained his stats about Death from the Internet but he only considered it a tool, a resource, an end unto itself. Jacob never thought it could provide the elusive answers that continually nagged at him.

Then he read an article in Wired about The Tor Project.

Tor stood for The Onion Router. It was free software that enabled anonymous communication by directing Internet traffic through more than seven thousand relays. It allowed the user's location and identity to be concealed so the person's privacy was protected and no one would ever know who was visiting which site or for what reason.

It's like you're invisible, the article had stated. Tor utilized a process called onion routing, so named because the identity of the user and the communication shared were all encrypted multiple times, like the layers of an onion. It was as if you were in an endless relay race and the baton kept changing size, shape and color each time it was passed along so the original possessor of the item could never be located or identified.

The government used and embraced Tor when it was introduced in the early 2000s and utilized it for the military to keep messages encrypted and secret, but like Frankenstein's monster, by 2004, Tor was corrupted and a dark underbelly was created that was hidden and anonymous. It was called the Deep Web or the Dark Net and it was where dangerous and robust trade occurred. It was growing at an alarming rate and had become home to skilled credit card scammers and those who forged currency and identity documents; weapons dealers, sellers of explosives and bomb making components (including uranium); hackers for hire, drug dealers, terrorist recruits; occult practitioners of every persuasion and their disciples who were fascinated by the dark arts; and seekers of extreme adult and child porn along with sex trafficking of every gender, age and fetish. The article had dramatically called the Dark Net the "hometown of the Bogeyman and any nightmare that causes you to wake up screaming. It's where seekers of the dark arts find other like-minded individuals. It's virtually endless, with the most hellish depictions and desires you'd ever not want to imagine. It's where every dirty secret goes."

The article concluded with a warning. "Don't take your morals to the Dark Net. If you do, you're asking to be sickened and offended." Or you could end up with all your Ashley Madison data dumped in the Deep Web, Jacob mused.

But what Jacob found so titillating about the article was the sense that anything goes in the Dark Net; down in that blackness, everything and anything could hide and was for sale or discovery.

Anything.

Somewhere in the Dark Net, Jacob suspected he'd find the answers about Death that he was seeking.

＊

Jacob thought access was going to be difficult and complicated but in the same way everyone was two clicks away from learning how to make a bomb or discovering hours of free porn, locating and gaining entrance to the Dark Net was easy. Step-by-step directions were readily available on YouTube and a simple Google search of the topic resulted in hundreds of thousands of answers.

He found his way into Tor via the Hidden Wiki—or the front door of Onionland—then he used TorDir to locate the TorLinks, which put him face to face with the Tor browser. Then he was stuck, so he called the woman who headed up IT at his office. Jacob worked from home most days as a subcontractor for an architecture design firm. He rendered their sketches into three-dimensional images so the clients had a better understanding where their money was going.

"First of all, drop all the 'Dark Net and Deep Web' stuff," Katherine told him dismissively. Jacob had been surprised she wasn't appalled or curious about his desire to visit the site.

"Why, am I using the terms wrong?"

Katherine was clacking away on her keyboards as she spoke. "No, but it just adds a lot of silly mystery and nonsense to it all. To make it simple, the Deep Web refers to all the web pages that the above ground search engines can't find. You enter through the Deep Web, and then you get down and dirty in the Dark Net."

"Got it," Jacob said.

"All you need is access to sites using the Tor Hidden Service Protocol and that works over the Tor network," she said. "You have the Tor browser, right?"

For the next thirty minutes, she walked him through what he was seeing on his screen and telling him where to click, what to download and what to be careful of. He had to create a throwaway email address each time he went into the Dark Net and was warned to use VirusScan before he downloaded something.

"Remember, it's going to be very slow going. Everything is bouncing around off volunteer servers so when you get on a forum, be patient when you ask a question. It'll take time for someone to respond to you."

"Okay," he said.

"And once you get down there, you will have access to some pretty sick stuff and dangerous people. That's why it's called HOE."

When he didn't reply, she said, "Hell on earth. You're a click away from some very bad places and groups, including terrorist recruiters, kiddie porn, kills for hire, and even worse."

"'*Even worse?*'"

"It's a sick world above ground," Katherine said. "As above, so below, right? Only more so when it's the Dark Net."

***

Like an overstuffed spreadsheet or, literally, a hopelessly tangled mesh, the Dark Net was a disorganized and chaotic mess.

Upon entrance, the forums and websites had vague names like DucknCover, PlanetHack, StoryVille and hundreds, maybe thousands, of others. Most of the links were dead or took too long to load so Jacob moved on. Many places stated their webpage was down but Katherine had told him that was just a ploy and to wait because most were on thirty second delays and would eventually appear if he was patient.

"It's all about being patient," she had explained to him. He wondered why she knew so much about the Dark Net, but since she had not questioned him, he did not query her.

The first evening, he explored for seven hours. He felt as if he had been dropped into the middle of a circus that was performing silently in the dark. He sensed something was going on, some form of activity, but he had no idea what it was or how to join in. He was an observer, a lurker, a voyeur, a troll who only watched what others posted. Most of what he saw was sex or drugs or weapons related. The porn sites were for the most part unwatchable, they were so harsh and cruel and not at all seductive to Jacob. Extreme forms of BDSM were everywhere, along with bestiality that included horses, dogs and even wild animals that had been drugged. Other sites stored images and promises that reminded him of walking past dark, filthy alleyways where there were sights and sounds that you didn't want in your head.

The majority of the Dark Net was not of interest to Jacob. He wasn't looking for sex or drugs or weapons or hit men, nor did he want to join ISIS or Boko Haram or the dozens of other terrorist groups that were swimming about like sharks. What he wanted was something that was even darker, but as the hours passed and the strain to his eyes caused them to burn and sting, he reluctantly abandoned his search.

The second evening he spent five hours visiting the forums and he began to make sense of some of what he was seeing. More than seventy percent of the sites were dead or playing possum and would not show signs of life unless you waited for thirty seconds. Then the latch—as it was called—would unlock and permit you into its depraved world. He was grateful Katherine had told him to be patient.

Jacob soon discovered that the Dark Net also had a trapdoor. He had thought it was a rumor, a place cryptically called the place for FK or forbidden knowledge. It all seemed a bit silly, like a boy's club in a tree house where old girlie magazine were lusted over, but he gradually came to understand that it was a real place. It was like a basement or cellar in the Dark Net, a deeper place of obscurities and secrets, and that was where Jacob was attempting to gain entrance. Everyone was suspicious of him but he persevered and latches were lifted and he was able to visit forums and sites with name like Pendragon, Kreafy's Library, Night Moth, Books of the Dead, Eclectic Artisans and the Sanctum of the Black Sun. He discovered that most of them were bogus in their claims of possessing secret manuscripts or having the ability to perform rituals for everlasting life. Simple Google searches revealed the scams employed in the Dark Net and Jacob was momentarily discouraged, even though he knew going in that most everyone simply wanted to make a buck, even if they claimed to be in league with Satan.

Everyone claimed to have a copy of The Necronomicon.

The third evening, he spent more than six hours visiting occult sites and was able to quickly tell the difference between the functioning ones and those that had closed or were inactive. Communication was concise in the forums. Words appeared one by one, not as complete sentences. Everything was seen in slow motion and it was all very dream-like.

The hours passed quickly. His eyes burned and stung. When he finally went to sleep a few hours before dawn, he had only nightmares, no dreams.

On the forth evening just before midnight, Jacob came across a site called DarkSeekers and those posting mentioned books he had never heard of: The Sixth and Seventh Book of Moses, The Spring Book, The Spiritual Shield, and others that apparently contained the secrets to obtain power over Death. He searched the forums until he found an active one.

He calmed himself, took a breath, and typed in, "Need power over Death."

His words appeared several seconds later.

Need. Power. Over. Death.

His left leg was shaking nervously under the computer desk.

Then, all at once, with no delay:

Who are you?

Jacob ignored the question. He had learned by watching that those who wanted to engage you in conversation were usually the scammers. He typed in:

Want. Ever. Lasting. Life.

Who are you?

Need. Power. Over. Death.

I have the other.

Confused, Jacob typed:

Ever. Lasting. Life?

A form of. Yes.

The response always came quickly and always in a complete sentence. Other forum questions rose up like a tide, flooding the board and pushing Jacob's questions and the answers out of his screen. You had to be patient but you also had to be fast. If someone wanted to connect with you, they employed a hook, which attached your threads. Whoever was communicated with Jacob had hooked him.

Again, Jacob typed:

Want. Ever. Lasting. Life.

Immediately: *I have a form of that. Who are you?*

Before Jacob could think how to respond, words appeared:

Do I know you?

Jacob leaned back, putting distance between himself and the computer screen. The conversation was unsettling and he was shaken by the questions. He decided to take a break. He stood up and stretched. He had been there at his desk for hours and needed to take a piss.

Minutes later when he returned to screen, the forum had been cleared. It was only his posts and the response from the other person. The last one remained, a question and almost an accusation: Do I know you?

Jacob typed:

Where'd. Everyone. Go?

I cleared the room. Who are you? Do I know you?

Who. Are. You? How. Do. You. Type. So. Fast?

Experience. What's your name?

Jacob was uneasy. Why did it matter what his name was?

What is your name? Do you want me to guess?

Jacob said, "No," to the computer screen and typed nothing.

Then:

Does your name begin with a J?

Jacob's mouth went dry. A tremor swept through his body as if a dowsing stick had found water and was pulling at it.

Are you a man or a woman?

Then:

You're a man. Your name begins with a J.

He felt a thick chill cascade down his back.

Then:

Why don't you answer me, Jacob?

The instant his name appeared, he pushed himself away from the desk with such terrified force that he nearly tipped over the chair he was sitting in. He stood, gasping, his legs weak and his arms trembling. He stared at the illuminated message: Why don't you answer me, Jacob?

Then, before any more words could appear, he escaped the site and slammed his laptop closed.

***

"That's very freaky," Katherine said the next day. "Seriously, dude, are you sure you didn't tell him or anyone your name? You sure you didn't leave a breadcrumb or post any pics that had data or code that they could trace back to you?"

"No," Jacob said. He had her on speakerphone at home and his laptop was on his desk, waiting for him. He hadn't slept much the night before, too unsettled over his experience yet also strangely compelled to return to the Dark Net. There was almost a sexual pull to it, like targeted porn that somehow knew all your obsessions and pleasure points and was created with only you in mind. He sensed that whatever inhuman thing was Down There—which is what he had started to call It, a place somewhere below the surface, a Rabbit Hole or a Hell Hole—It not only knew his name but It could help him obtain what he was after.

"You're going back, aren't you?" she said.

He didn't need to answer.

"That's what happens to people when they visit that place," she said. He could hear her tapping away at her keyboard. It was the sound of rustling animal feet padding about. "People have this need to go back again and again and again. It's like porn."

"Yeah," he said, staring at his computer screen, itching to go back Down There. "But I wanted to check with you first to see what you thought. Maybe it was just a very, very creepy wild guess that he knew my name."

"Could be," she said absently. Tap, click, rustle, pad. "But people say..."

He waited.

"...there's a lot of weird shit that goes on down there and weird, powerful people."

"Powerful people?"

She stopped typing. He knew he had her full attention.

"Because it's totally anonymous, anybody can go down there and no one will ever know who they are," she said. "Or what they are. Famous people or super rich people, you know? It sort of takes on a life of its own, know what I mean?"

Yes, he did know exactly what she meant.

"So be careful, Jacob, okay? It's not a nice place to visit and you certainly wouldn't want to live there, right?"

After he ended the call, he went back down the Rabbit Hole. It was much easier and faster finding his way to the trap door and from there, into the basements and cellars. Many of the forums he had looked at before were gone or no longer active. That was the way with the Dark Net, it morphed into something new every few minutes so it was constantly changing and deleting and recreating itself. It was perfect for those who wanted to remain undetected and unknown, and frustrating for those who wanted to find them.

DarkSeekers was gone as expected, and Jacob was relieved. He spent an hour skipping around forums until he came to one called GreatAdepts&TrainedSeers. It was rabid with activity and there was a fierce amount of subject matter posted that intrigued him: Need HELP!! Deciphering the mutterings of dead shamans; my journey to katabasis; freedom from interment!!!; Need location of ritual conjuring pit!

The postings were slow of course, and plodding, but there were so many of them that they appeared as a flurry of statements that blurred before his eyes. Like snowflakes that quickly piled up, requests appeared on the site and then were lost as a blizzard of new ones appeared. Desires and pleas were repeated endlessly, words over a slow motion waterfall.

Jacob finally dove in and typed:

Need. Power. Over. Death.

No one responded. Other messages piled up like floodwaters.

Then:

I can help you.

Proof? Jacob posted, not wanting to waste any time.

I've done it before.

Proof!

Jacob had learned to be more aggressive Down Under. It was very much a cash grab environment. He who hesitates would be lost in the pile-up of posts.

He was about to leave and try another site when the poster hooked him and wrote:

China. Tomorrow. 10 a.m.

How. Will. I. Find. You. Again? Jacob posted.

I'll find you.

***

He spent three more hours in the Rabbit Hole, but received no other responses. After he logged off at 2 a.m., Jacob slept in fits and starts, his mind occupied with thoughts about China and the type of proof he could expect.

The next morning, he watched the news but nothing was mentioned about China. In the light of day, above ground and far away from the depths of the Dark Net, Jacob was forced to admit it was all a bit crazy. Someone was just toying with him, another troll from Down There.

He turned off the TV at 10:30 a.m. He went to Google. He typed in China. He hit news as a sub-search. Five headlines popped up. Jacob read three of them:

> *Chinese boy thought dead awakens in morgue*
> *"Resurrected" child in China stuns doctors, delights family*
> *Dead boy returns to life; Chinese physicians baffled*

The stories had all been posted at 10 a.m. He read through them all and then clicked on the follow-up stories and the corrections that were made. An hour later, he was as convinced as the astonished reporters and doctors who had written and were quoted in the stories. Apparently a bus had hit a 3-year-old boy and his mother in the village of Cuandixia. The driver had lost control of the vehicle after suffering from an epileptic seizure. No one in the bus had died, but the mother and son had been pronounced dead at the scene of the accident. The next morning, the

78

bodies were being prepared for burial when the boy opened his eyes. He had fully recovered but his mother did not.

China. Tomorrow. 10 a.m.

Jacob immediately went back Down There and searched for the forum GreatAdepts&TrainedSeers but it was no longer active. Two hours into his search, he came across a brand new site, established seconds earlier. A shiver swept through him.

JacobsLadder.

The forum was empty. No activity, no posts. He was the first:

China. Came. True.

Instantly, the reply unfurled across the screen.

Of course it did.

What. Now?

Life everlasting, life over Death.

Yes. How?

Lean in.

Jacob automatically leaned in closer to the screen.

Closer.

Why. Am. I. Doing. This?

Life everlasting, life over Death.

Feeling foolish but curious, wondering if he was being pranked, Jacob hunched over until he was a few inches from the screen. The text was big and bright and seemed to pulsate, he was so close to it. All around the border of the forum, he could see shifting movements. The murky shapes reminded him of pollywogs, large heads with thin bodies that darted about. Of course, there was nothing there, nothing moving; it was just the illusion that occurred with his face so close to the screen.

Forehead on screen.

What? Why?

Contact needed for life over death. Now and forever, correct?

Yes. Now. And. Forever.

Jacob sighed. Whoever or Whatever was communicating with him had managed to raise the little boy from the dead, so It certainly had proven it had power over Death. There was no reason to doubt It or not do as It asked.

Jacob adjusted himself so he could press his forehead against the screen. The words in front of him distorted and blurred. He waited and was again aware of movements in his peripheral vision, like thick black eels aimlessly searching for a meal, but now they appeared to be in his room, repositioning themselves behind the computer. Impossible, of course.

It sort of takes on a life of its own, he recalled Katherine saying.

He was conscious of his breathing; it had become haggard and thick, his lungs were struggling to fill with air. His back began to ache from the awkward position. His throat tightened and he felt queasy. His brow remained pressed against the screen. His chest and shoulders started to tremble in discomfort.

This is ridiculous, Jacob thought. They are probably filming me right now, the idiot with his head pressed against the screen.

He abruptly straightened up and cried out in pain. The computer screen came with him, his forehead still attached to it. The texture of the monitor had suddenly turned thick and gummy, like Vaseline with a solid underneath. He tried to push it away but it was firmly affixed and gripped his brow; the skin would tear away if he removed the screen.

Jacob carefully returned to his original position so the computer was flat on his desk and his shoulders were hunched over it. He closed his eyes since staring at the monitor and the distorted words had begun to give him a headache. He sensed that there were images that were beginning to move about behind him in the room.

He was breathing deeply and still felt sick to his stomach. His neck and shoulders ached under the strain of having his forehead pressed against the screen. Wearily, he opened his eyes. Surprisingly, his words were no longer blurry. They could be easily read. In fact, his vision was now perfect even though he was still attached forehead-to-screen to the computer monitor.

Now and forever.

"Yes," he said, helplessly. "Life over death, now and forever."

Now?

"Yes," he whispered, almost weeping he was in such discomfort. "I want it to begin now."

Now and forever.

He read the words on the monitor.

Then the screen went black.

He fell forward. The computer had vanished. He quickly straightened up, the pain in his neck and shoulders eased.

His room was in darkness. Disoriented, he stood up, rotating his shoulders, trying to determine where the desk lamp was. Had the computer really disappeared? He reached around into the blackness. The air felt thicker and heavier, almost as if he was under water. He sensed he was not alone in the room and perceived that he was advancing toward an opposing force.

He paused. He swallowed and heard the thick saliva crackle. *Are my eyes opened*, he wondered. *Am I awake or is this a dream?*

Feeling about blindly, he sensed a vast expanse around him. Where had the room gone? The ground had softened and was no longer the floorboards of his home. It was now earth, slanted and uneven, like walking on mounds of sand.

"Hello?"

A dense but fluid silence seemed to lean in at the sound of his voice.

He called out again. He sounded muffled, like he was speaking from under a blanket.

"Is anyone there?"

Jacob.

He didn't actually hear his name called, he intuited it. Somewhere around him, there was a manifestation of Something that knew who he was and it was acknowledging he was there.

"Who is there?"

I am the one with the form of what you wanted.

"Power over death? Life everlasting?"

A form of that. Yes.

The air about him was now thick, warm, and moist, like a sauna. Everything remained black and he was sightless. He peered through the dark, squinting into its midst. *Maybe it was like the long tunnel that dead people say they go through before they reach the other side,* he thought. *Am I in a dark tunnel? And will there be a light breaking forth?*

Jacob eagerly continued forward, his arms extended in the blackness, his feet stumbling at times over the rocky earth.

His footfalls on the ground crunched and at times slurped in the mud or guck he was walking on; a swamp or mud patch? Where had he wandered? The atmosphere congealed, tightening in on itself, and he could almost feel the darkness he was walking into.

He tripped and cried out as he landed on his back. He thought he had felt Something grab his ankle. It would have pulled him away if he hadn't fallen, but now Something monstrous pressed down on him. Were there two entities stalking him? This one had the shape and feel of gravity or the blackness that he was now swimming in. It was animal-like—he sensed there was a snout—but there was an overall weight that was bearing down on him, not the legs of any mammal. It was massive and sludge-like. He didn't struggle; he knew it would be useless. The force on top of him, having subdued him, seemed to quickly seep into his body, invading his pores with its embodiment. A transformation? Jacob wondered with hope. An empowerment? Was it happening now? Was he being endued with the Power Over Death?

Gradually, as he lay there panting, the black night thinned into gray, a mist that then parted like a secret veil. Was this the light? It was like a slow dawn breaking out, shadows stretching until they splintered and dissolved. The area around him was still a dreary shadow land, void of color, but he could now vaguely make out shapes. He was in a forest or a rocky place with tall sarsens all around him that reached far into the sky, or whatever was above him. The illumination was more twilight than dawn and it shimmered, struggling, as if held in place by a more powerful unseen presence.

Now and forever.

Dazed but serene, Jacob knew it was about to begin: It was The Forever, the Power Over Death. He now had the empowerment to never yield to The End or the Cruel Thing that had taken his parents and sister and grandparents and wife and stepdaughter. He would be forever free of What consumed more than 153,000 each day, free from Death, which obliterated 56 million lives each year.

He was in a new world, an afterlife of life that was both now and forever more. Anticipation welled up inside of Jacob as he sensed he was in the presence of God or a god or every god that had the power to rule over All, even the Power of Death.

Above him, the sky-like firmament began to waver and flicker in the same way the twilight had, as if it was distressed by its position or purpose. A struggle seemed to be occurring, one world pressing into and against another. Cloud-like imageries appeared like ink swirling about in liquid and they imploded upon themselves overhead, like dull and slow-paced fireworks.

For a moment, he was in awe at what he was witnessing, and then the cloudy images began to refine themselves, and with clarity came realization. Jacob, still immobilized by the invisible force, could not look away as sights and sounds unfurled in the heavens.

The first image was of a young girl, no more than five, who was being viciously molested by her father. Her screams and cries for help echoed harshly around Jacob. He was unable to cover his ears or look away from what was occurring. He was restrained on the ground, paralyzed by the vast, blasphemous weight that rested on his chest and arms, securing him in Its embrace.

The second image was a torture victim with more than half of his face torn off. He was bound in a chair and a woman in a hideous red and pink housecoat was flaying the skin off of his body as he shrieked and withered in the chair.

The third image was of an elderly man being dismembered by a group of teenagers who taunted and mocked his cries for mercy.

Each image appeared for only a few seconds, just long enough for the horrific incident to sicken and register with Jacob, and then another replaced it. He knew they were all from the Dark Net, things he had chosen not to look at as he had scrolled through the forums in search of the Power Over Death, of Life Everlasting.

I have a form of that.

HOE Katherine had called it. Hell on earth.

Jacob had found what he was looking for, or at least a form of it.

Now and forever. Life everlasting.

Helplessly, Jacob could only watch, and take it all in.

END

The Hawk, The Hand, and The Hell-Eyed Man
Matt Shoen

Ollette sat in the terraced beer garden of the Schaefer Pothouse, sipping iced tea and hoping a killer would walk by. The beer garden overlooked the Malting Corridor, a bustling avenue running through the heart of Cellee, and was one of the better places to scan a crowd. Ollette stared at hundreds of faces as they passed by to go day drinking, or fish. Each person had the potential to be the killer, walking around, enjoying his afternoon, unaware he was being hunted. That was how Ollette liked it, hovering in the shadows, stalking criminals when they thought they were safe. She remembered any face she'd seen, always had. Hawk eyes, that's what her partners Ludin and Arrus called her ability, and her hawk eyes had always come through, until this murderer.

The problems started with Arrus. Ollette's abilities were uncanny, his were unnatural. Arrus could see the final minutes of a person's life, thumb through their death and describe everything he saw to Ludin who sketched a picture for Ollette. It was an efficient system so long as she had a face to hunt.

For the past week Ollette had been working their best sketch, a profile of a smooth cheek and pierced ear with a gold ring, seen through the dying eyes of the killer's sixth and latest victim.

They'd been hopeful. The sketch ruled out most of the men being rounded up and beaten for confessions by the boot squads. Those men, rough faced immigrants working by the waterfront as grain and coal shovelers, hadn't been Ollette's prime suspects anyways. She'd seen immigrant murders, gory bar fights, or robberies gone wrong, ending with someone getting knifed. The killer didn't care about anything aside from anonymity. Money was left behind, jewelry too, and each murder was brutally precise. A hand over the mouth to stifle the screams, followed by one swift slash to the throat, the body left behind for someone to discover in the morning, the victim never seeing her killer.

Ollette gave up the hunt at sundown and left the pothouse, cutting through a maze of alleyways until she reached Ludin's building. It was three stories and owned by a grocer who rented the attic to Ludin and let him grow vegetables in back. Ollette carefully stepped around the plants and went up the back stair to the cramped nook Ludin called home. She'd tried convincing Ludin to move since his apartment was their de facto office. It drove Ollette mad working in the narrow flat, but her house was a constant mess of toys and dirt tracked in by her sons and Arrus in a grimy hole above a dive bar. Until she convinced Ludin to move they were stuck sitting around his kitchen table, bumping elbows every few minutes.

"Ludin, let me in!" yelled Ollette after she tried the door and found it latched. Minutes later Ludin appeared, fingers black with grease from his charcoal pencils, and smudges beneath his sharp green eyes.

"No luck?" he grunted, ushering Ollette into the kitchen where a few chicken thighs were hissing on the stove.

"Nothing," sighed Ollette, "everyone wears earrings and they all look the same. I spotted one after another that could've been a match, but none of them felt right. After a while I got paranoid that the killer took his earring out.

"Arrus said it didn't..."

"I know, I'm just tired," said Ollette.

"Do you want something to eat? Some water?"

"Sure, Sigmund probably didn't cook enough for dinner. Theo and Aldo are getting so big, they eat constantly and Sigmund hordes money like we're living in that dump above Hentz's. The man has seventy hogs and sweats buying a pound of onions," Ollette laughed.

"He's not used to making money, afraid it'll dry up," said Ludin, scattering salt across the pan. "That's the benefit of our work; we never make money so we've never had to worry about losing it."

Ollette rolled her eyes as Ludin grabbed a glass and filled it with water from a bucket.

"Thank you," she said, as Ludin went back to prodding the chicken.

Ollette took a drink and looked around the kitchen, which was filled with Ludin's drawings and paintings. There was always something new to see. Even the old paintings sometimes revealed new aspects of themselves which helped Ollette decompress. When she was stressed, Ollette enjoyed coming to Ludin's apartment, the paintings were about the only thing she liked about the place.

"You all right?" Ludin asked, putting out silverware and plates.

"Not really," said Ollette. "I've looked for that earring all week; I've sat in every beer garden and park, walked down every street, and come up with nothing."

Ludin nodded and served Ollette before dishing some chicken for himself.

"I don't see how we're going to prevent another murder."

"I don't know either," said Ludin quietly, "we just don't have enough right now."

"It's hard on Arrus."

"It's always hard on Hell-eyes."

Ludin sighed and stared out the window at the garden where a few hummingbirds were having a night feed before zipping off to sleep. He'd paint them later.

"We'd both do anything for Arrus, but he has his role and we have ours."

"And our roles require us to sit and wait for another woman to get her throat slashed," said Ollette miserably.

"So it seems," said Ludin, taking a bite. He suddenly didn't have much of an appetite, just an urge to paint.

"I know I spend too much time thinking about the victims," Ollette said, "I've seen the faces of every family member, every line of their grief. It's getting heavy Ludin. Every night I think about the new faces I might have to see in the morning, the horror, tears."

"It's not your fault Ollette."

"It doesn't matter if it's my fault. I CAN'T forget faces, I can't push them aside. All the families, they're piling up. I can't take a break; bury their sadness under better memories. I'm not sure it would even be right to."

Ollette shuddered, wiping a couple tears away. Ludin leaned over and wrapped his arms around her.

"I was hoping you'd make me feel better," laughed Ollette after a minute, "Now I feel like I've just made you sad."

"You and Arrus have the burden of seeing things. I just draw," replied Ludin, forcing a smile. "Confidant, therapist whatever you call it. It's what I'm here for right?"

"Yea," said Ollette, forcing herself to smile. "Another time though, I need to go home."

Ollette stood up, wiping the tears away. "Thank you for dinner."

"Of course," said Ludin, giving Ollette another hug.

"Grab Arrus and come by tomorrow morning, we'll pick over what he saw in case we missed something," added Ludin, trying to be hopeful.

"Sure, it alright if I bring the boys?"

"Yea, they can play in the garden."

"Alright. See you tomorrow."

***

Ollette went down the back stairs and into the quiet streets. She thought about picking up something for tomorrows dinner, but the grocers she liked were closed up for the night, all that remained were fruit and vegetable stands whose produce had gone soft from sitting in the sun all afternoon. Sigmund could get some peppers and lime on his way home from the pig farm.

Ollette sighed. Ludin was just making up busy work until the next murder, trying to keep her and Arrus emotionally afloat. Ollette hated the case; couldn't wait for it to be over. She wanted to stop glaring into crowds, always on edge, looking for an earring and cheek profile that would tear off the killer's mask. All the women who'd died, Ollette remembered herself at their age. Right when she'd met Sigmund, found Ludin and Arrus, and finally felt like there was purpose to her powers. Her memory stopped being a curse and Ollette realized what she could do. Six young women would never have that; they'd never be more than drunken girls murdered in the darkness.

"When we catch you I'm going to take a long vacation," Ollette muttered. She'd sit with Sigmund and drink, take Theo and Aldo to the pier and let all the horror stricken faces slip into the background.

Before she could take another step someone grabbed Ollette from behind, clamping a hand over her mouth. Ollette covered her throat and a knife slashed the back of her hand, cutting it to the bone. She screamed into the killer's choking hand, twisting and squirming, blood running down the front of her shirt as the killer tried grappling her to the ground.

She tried biting his hand and stomping his toes as he danced around, trying to slash her throat. Ollette grabbed his wrist, holding the knife in front of her, instantly memorizing everything about the ugly little dirk as the killer tried breaking her grip. She held on, backing him against a wall and delivered a nasty kick to his shin, sending a spasm through the killer's arm. He grunted, stumbling to a knee, and Ollette surged forward, trying to run. She wasn't far from home!

A meaty fist drilled her in the temple. She staggered. There was someone else with the killer! Ollette lost her grip and the killer opened her throat.

She didn't feel pain, just lightheaded, and then a moment of clarity. As things were going dark she jerked her head backwards, nailing the killer with a head-butt. He dropped her and Ollette fell forward, landing on her back, looking straight up at the killer.

He didn't try hiding his face and Ollette smiled. So this was him, and he had a little posse circled around him, grinning. Ludin and Arrus would know the killer's face instantly; they didn't need her.

Things began to darken and Ollette felt tremors in her fingers travel up her arms. She was scared, what would she do without Sigmund and her children? They were fading from her memory like flowers wilting in the sun. She was forgetting things! Ollette closed her eyes and focused on remembering everyone she loved in the last moments before she died.

***

A battering ram, or at least that's what it sounded like, woke Ludin. He stumbled from bed, past the painting of hummingbirds he'd finished at three in the morning, into the kitchen.

"I'm coming!" he snarled. The door stopped rattling and Ludin took a moment to douse his head with water, before opening the door.

It was Karl, his contact in the Brewmasters, the merchants who'd hired him, Arrus, and Ollette to catch the killer. Karl only came for two reasons. Either he had been tasked with delivering threats, or bringing Ludin to the scene of the next murder.

"Do you want to come in," Ludin asked guardedly.

"No. I need you to come with me," growled Karl. Another murder, the seventh killing Ollette had been dreading.

"Just give me a minute to grab my stuff," said Ludin, hurrying back to his bedroom.

"Be quick! We're trying to get this body off the street before too many people see it!" shouted Karl. Ludin sighed, packing away paper and a few pieces of charcoal before setting up his easel. He'd make color sketches in the afternoon for Ollette so she could scope the streets.

"Hurry up," growled Karl as Ludin passed through the kitchen and stopped to grab a piece of bread.

"Shut up," said Ludin, staring Karl right in the face, watching him turn a bruised purple. Karl was a peon and it was too early in the morning, on a day Ludin needed to be sharp, to listen to him.

Karl sputtered empty threats until Ludin got bored and walked away, leaving the Brewmaster peon to run after him like a sulking child.

Once he caught up, Karl tried hurrying Ludin down the Malting Corridor. Ludin ignored his huffs and constant glances and focused on mentally retracing the curve of the killer's ear and cheek. Hopefully, he'd be able to put together a composite sketch for Ollette from Arrus's newest vision and what they already had. Ludin wanted to be done with the case. Ollette was right, it was killing them.

"We're almost there," said Karl, though Ludin didn't need to be told, the circle of boot squad foot soldiers and whispering ladies was a dead giveaway. The cordon parted and Ludin saw Arrus sitting beside a shrouded body, head buried in his hands.

Ludin sighed. It was always hardest on Arrus.

"Be quick, so we can get the body off the streets," muttered Karl as the guards collapsed back into position, ignoring the shouts of a dozen housewives eager for gossip.

"Go play with your boot squad goons," growled Ludin, earning a few glares. He didn't care. The boot squads put boots to whomever they wanted without repercussions. They'd earned their name.

Ludin sat next to Arrus, putting a hand on his shoulder, "what'd you see buddy?" Ludin asked. Arrus didn't say a word, so Ludin gave it a minute, massaging his shoulders, loosening tension that riveted Arrus's back.

"Talk me through it," Ludin whispered, ignoring an angry look from Karl, "We'll sit here as long as it takes, alright?"

"It's Ollette!" Arrus blurted out.

"She's not here yet," Ludin said, the words slipping out thoughtlessly.

"No," choked Arrus, pointing at the shroud. Confused, Ludin pulled back the cloth and there was Ollette, dead in the street, her eyes gouged out.

It was like someone pulled out his soul and splattered it on the ground, letting it run off into the drain. There were feelings he'd never dreamt of suddenly looming up inside him, bludgeoning the foolish part of him that tried to comprehend that Ollette had been murdered. Emotions beat on him, screaming that it wasn't her, it wasn't possible, she wasn't dead, Ollette wasn't dead!

It was just a couple blocks from his apartment to her house, a five minute walk she'd taken thousands of times without trouble. He'd let her go alone, never believing it could happen to Ollette. He looked at the shroud. Arrus had pulled it back over Ollette's face. Ludin begged the cloth to rise and fall with Ollette's breathing, but it refused to move, refused to do more than mask the horror of Ollette's final moments. Her damn eyes pulled out.

Ludin swallowed with difficulty and dug around in his pocket. He still had charcoal, and his sketch pad was crushed against his arm. He took a ragged breath and went over to Arrus.

"Are you ready, Arrus?" Ludin asked, getting his tools squared away.

"I can't."

"Yes you can," said Ludin, "You've got to."

"She's our friend, I can't ... I can't watch her die."

Ludin wrapped Arrus in a tight hug, "This is going to be harder for you than me, but if Ollette saw his face .... She might have given us everything we need to end this!"

Arrus gave the shroud a hard look before gently pulling back the cloth. Ludin turned away, he couldn't look at her mutilated body, it made his fingers quiver. He couldn't have that.

"Tell me when you're ready," muttered Arrus, putting both hands on Ollette's temples.

"Go."

The air grew dense and Ludin felt the cold of death seep out of Arrus as he relived Ollette's final moments.

"She was walking when he grabbed her," Arrus began. Around them the guards began to look back and a few wandered over to watch, drawn by morbid fascination.

"He slit her throat," gurgled Arrus, "he caught her deep and she fell, turning."

Ludin leaned forward ready to begin sketching. Instead Arrus let go and the cold hellwind was sucked back into him.

"She was talking to me," whispered Arrus, "said she loved me, and loved you."

"She wanted us to tell Sigmund and the boys she loved them."

Ludin was silent.

"She just thought about how much she loves us, that's all she thought at the end."

"She didn't see his face," Arrus whispered at last.

"Nothing at all?" Ludin gasped.

"Nothing."

"God damn it!" Ludin sobbed, they had nothing!

"I'll go tell Sigmund," choked Arrus.

"Right."

"I'll come to your place when I'm done."

Arrus staggered past the cordon where the crowd had begun dispersing. Soon it was just Ludin and a few guards standing over Ollette's body, Karl off to the side fidgeting. For once, the boot squads were respectful and let Ludin take his time. After half an hour though, they nudged him aside and took Ollette's body to the undertaker, leaving Ludin cradling a blank piece of paper.

He got home eventually and sat on the back stairway, glaring at his sketchpad. Ludin began drawing; reproducing all the details of the killer's face, straining to turn the awful profile into a clear image. He worked without realizing time, starting and stopping, tearing out worthless sketches and covering his stairway in crumpled paper. There were no eyes to work with, no mouth, no nose, not even a hairline! He couldn't find the killer even with all those details! He needed Ollette!

Ludin threw his remaining charcoal pencils against the wall. He had to do something, but there was nothing he could do. Of all the people the killer could've chosen, he picked the only woman capable of catching him.

Ludin went inside and sat in his kitchen, thinking about the killer to keep from thinking about Ollette. The other victims had been found closer to the pothouses and beer gardens; Ollette was the outlier, killed in a busy residential neighborhood, a risky neighborhood where people walked around at odd hours. Further, all the other victims were young women stumbling home by themselves along dead quiet streets, easy targets.

Ludin stiffened. It hadn't been a random killing. The killer went after Ollette, not because she was a woman, or because she was alone, but because she was Ollette. Most people in Cellee didn't know about Arrus, Ludin, and Ollette, it was their advantage.

The killer knew. He had to.

Heavy footsteps in the hallway interrupted Ludin's thoughts. They didn't match the light step of the grocer's wife. Ludin grabbed a knife and tensed as a piece of paper slid beneath the door. The person stomped away and Ludin waited until the echo of the last footstep faded before grabbing the note.

He wasn't a popular man; if people wanted Ludin they just came and got him. Nobody sent him notes or invitations of any sort. Yet, when he unfolded the paper there was an invitation for Arrus and himself to visit Fredrick Haarmann's mansion.

Fredrick Haarmann, a name Ludin knew more than a face he recognized. There was no reason for this man to invite Ludin to his mansion, well almost no reason. Haarmann was president of the Brewmasters, the man behind the boot squads, and peons like Karl. He knew about Ollette's death, he'd probably known about it hours before anyone else. The invitation was probably a Brewmaster formality required to cancel their contract.

Ludin tore up the note and threw it in the stove just as someone knocked on his back door.

"It's me," said Arrus. Ludin opened up and Arrus, face irrigated with tears, stepped inside.

"How is Sigmund?" Ludin asked.

"He doesn't know how to tell Theo and Aldo their mother died, kept asking me what he should say. I don't know what he should tell them. I didn't know what to tell him Ludin."

"I feel like I've been stabbed," Arrus whispered, "she was so calm when she died; I wish I could give that calm to Sigmund, but how can I? I can't even take it for myself."

Ludin shook his head, he had no clue.

"She did see the killer's face," said Arrus.

"Why didn't you tell me?!"

"Because you'd tear your hair out if you knew! There's nothing we can do. He's untouchable."

"Tell me who it is," Ludin snarled.

"You really want to know?! Johan Haarmann."

"The Brewmaster's son?"

"Yea," hissed Arrus. "Untouchable."

"He's got at least two boot squad goons helping him, I couldn't tell you earlier in case one of them was part of the cordon."

"Right," said Ludin as he dug through his stove retrieving the paper scraps he'd tossed in.

"What's this?" Arrus asked as Ludin put the note back together.

"We were just invited to Frederick Haarmann's mansion."

"Why would the Brewmaster want us?" Arrus asked, eyes narrowing. "Do you think he's involved?"

"What's his motivation? The killings only hurt his business."

"What if it's a trap?"

"It's Frederick's signature, I recognize the way he shapes letters."

"The little sonofabitch," hissed Arrus, "We'll go in and kill him, beg Frederick for mercy once we're done," snarled Arrus, grabbing a knife.

"We'd be cut down before we got close."

"What then?!"

"We'll go see what Frederick wants," Ludin said. It was a shaky plan, but Ludin was punch drunk. He didn't have a better idea.

***

Just before sunset, Ludin and Arrus tramped down the back stairs and into the street. Both carried kitchen knives tucked into their pants. They'd die pulling the blades, but walking into the mansion unarmed seemed like something overconfident fools would do, and neither man considered himself a fool, or confident.

They were caught up in their own thoughts and barely noticed as the winding streets walled with houses thinned out, replaced by sandstone mansions and manicured lawns. Each mansion had snootily dressed gatemen shooting the breeze with sharp-eyed guards; men who'd aged out of the boot squads, but still enjoyed putting boots to the odd homeless person or drunk.

The Haarmann Mansion was near the top of the hill overlooking Cellee. Ludin and Arrus approached the gatehouse and were ushered into a verdant garden filled with flowering bushes and artfully trimmed hops with bright green seed cones drooping from their stems.

A woman led Ludin and Arrus inside. She was friendly, asking questions which they dutifully answered, all while keeping their eyes moving, memorizing everything they saw in case it became useful later.

The woman stopped in front of a varnished cherry door and ushered Ludin and Arrus in with a bow. They smiled, faking their gratitude. In the room, two guards were posted behind a desk where a man sat, staring at them.

Ludin had seen Frederick Haarmann's face on barrels of beer, proclamations, and paintings hung above bars. He'd even seen it scrawled on bathroom walls. The living face was different. It lay still, like a leopard waiting to ambush a rabbit, knowing that even if it did not succeed on the first strike all it needed to do was wait. Another opportunity would come running down the track.

"Sit down," Frederick said, motioning to a pair of upholstered chairs in front of his desk.

"I believe there's something we need to speak about and there's no point dancing around the issue. Your partner is dead," said Haarmann.

"She was our friend," Arrus said, his voice shaking. Ludin put a hand on Arrus's shoulder as Haarmann gave them a strange look.

"Emotions aside," he said, coughing quietly, "without your hawk things will be very difficult, almost impossible."

"We'll manage," said Ludin.

"You've been put under contract to succeed, not to manage and right now you cannot succeed. You're blind men trying to play darts."

Frederick Haarmann shook his head, drinking a dark brown beer from his stein. "The Brewmasters motto is in Gottes Paradies werden Hopfen und Malz, do you know what that means?"

Ludin and Arrus shook their heads and Haarmann took another drink, "In old Geren it means in God's paradise be hops and malt. Hops and malt, the blood of beer. Beer is the blood of Cellee and right now this killer has opened our city's veins. People will not drink if they think they will die, women especially are so easily spooked, the killer could be caught tonight and they'd spend the rest of the month cowering to home afraid of his ghost," Haarmann growled, taking another drink.

Ludin swallowed his fury and looked over at Arrus whose hands were shaking.

"I contracted you three because your powers... well they spoke for themselves, but now three have become two and two can't stop this vile scum."

"What do you propose," asked Ludin, fighting to keep his tone polite.

"I proposed cancelling your contract and flooding the city with guards, but my son had a different idea, one you'll appreciate because it keeps you employed."

Ludin thought Arrus would bite off his tongue as the cherry doors swung open admitting a clean shaven young man with a simple gold earring in his right ear. Completely nondescript, except Ludin had drawn it two dozen times. The knife in his pants was suddenly hot and Ludin wanted to use it. The guards would kill him; they'd grind him into mush, but he wanted it bad.

"My son pointed something out to me. The killing of your partner looks random, but really it's too convenient she died. The Brewmasters are a united organization, but only we knew of your efforts. There must be a traitor. While he is no hawk, Johan knows the Brewmasters intimately. He will help you catch the killer," said Frederick with a smile, smacking his son on the back.

Johan stepped forward and offered a hand to Ludin and Arrus. In a split second Ludin reached out, took Johan's hand, and shook it. He smiled, forcing his lips to curve up.

The knife would go right into Johan's heart and the guards would kill him. The men who'd helped Johan murder Ollette would go free.

"It'll be good to work with you," said Johan, breaking the contact and shaking Arrus's hand. Ludin sat down, his skin burning. They all needed to go down.

"Well," said Frederick, "I suppose there's no other business keeping us. Tomorrow you three will start working to find out who's betrayed the Brewmasters." Frederick said, stepping around his son, bumping the boy on his way out.

"Good evening to you," he said as the guards ushered Ludin and Arrus down the hall.

***

"I'm going to go get real drunk now," muttered Arrus, after they'd rejoined the bustle around the Malting Corridor.

"I need your help..."

"No you don'! I see things and you figure out what to do with them, that's how it's always been."

"Things are different!"

"I had to watch Ollette get murdered today! I felt the killer's hand pressed against her mouth, and then I shook that hand with a smile stitched to my face. I could smell Ollette's blood. I'm going to get real drunk now and pass out, if you don't object."

Arrus sighed, "You're better at this Ludin. You can find a way to outsmart him. I won't add a damn thing so let me get drunk, please."

I'll have someone get you tomorrow morning," Ludin said quietly. There was nothing he could do but let Arrus cope and hope he didn't wake up too hungover to function.

"Tomorrow afternoon," grunted Arrus, leaving to blackout his trauma.

Ludin sighed and went home where he lit a few candles and sat in the kitchen staring off into the darkness. His fingers started itching for charcoal and paper so he drew absently, connecting lines, shading corners, and creating an ugly mess on the paper while he thought.

They needed Johan to admit his guilt. He and Arrus could present their evidence to Frederick, but the man would not be convinced until there was a confession, a very public unforced confession. How to get it though?

He glanced at the doodle and jumped. He'd sketched Ollette's face, perfectly represented, except her eyes. He'd left black hollows where the eyes belonged, hollows carved out by Johan Haarmann.

Ludin crumpled the drawing and threw it in the cold stove.

"Sonofabitch," he muttered, splashing water on his face.

Ludin took out another piece of paper. He wouldn't draw Ollette like that. He started a drawing things he'd never paid attention to, the mole on her throat, the tiny scar below her right ear. When he got to her eyes Ludin couldn't remember how they looked, all he saw were black hollows, clotted with blood.

The second drawing shared the fate of the first and Ludin struck a match, setting both on fire. Had he imprinted Ollette's final visage over all the happy times? Why though? He could remember everything else, but her eyes had vanished.

"Sonofabitch," Ludin snarled, feeding more paper into the fire, watching the flames roar.

Ludin let the paper burn down to twisted black ash, plunging the kitchen into darkness. He closed his eyes and the darkness became absolute.

He tried remembering Ollette's eyes, but couldn't. They were gone, taken from him just like Ollette. Where were her eyes? Why had Johan taken them when he'd been content to just murder his other victims? Why did he mutilate Ollette?

An idea pierced Ludin's skull, burrowing into his brain. Johan had taken Ollette's eyes. Ollette's eyes! There didn't need to be a confession.

***

Ludin waited until the noon bell rang to send for Arrus who came, red faced and shaking, a little dried vomit stuck to his shirt.

"What's the plan?"

"You're going to show Johan a new aspect of your vision, one he's never heard of," said Ludin.

"Go on," the Hell-Eyed man said.

***

97

As the afternoon wore on Arrus felt his hangover subside. This was his blessing. Though he got drunk far too quickly and hungover far too often, the hangovers rarely lasted and were never debilitating. This was good because he'd never needed a drink so badly.

He'd been paralyzed when the boot squad grunts showed him Ollette's body. Watching her struggle and die, then console him from beyond the grave only made things worse. She'd been dying, looking up at Johan's smirk, the last thing she'd ever see, and thought of him, Ludin, and her family and been at peace. He'd told this to Sigmund for whom it brought a kernel of peace. It did no such thing for Arrus. He didn't want to think of Ollette as dead, peaceful or not, he wanted her alive.

Arrus wiped away a tear and looked down the street. Ludin had sent a message to Johan telling him to come to the office at two. Around five minutes to three Johan appeared, trailed by a pair of trolls from the boot squads.

"Where is your partner?" Johan asked, smiling nonchalantly.

"We don't need him for this," grunted Arrus. He started walking and Johan fell in beside him.

"Where are we going?" asked Johan cheerfully.

Arrus was silent so Johan asked him again.

"Ollette's house, I need to watch her death one more time."

"That must be hard, she was your friend, I can't imagine."

"We do what we must," muttered Arrus, rounding the corner onto Ollette's street.

"My father always says things like that. We do what we must for hops and malt," Johan said, mimicking Frederick.

"Anything is permitted so long as it brings money to Haarmann coffers and beer to Cellee. He says that all the time."

Arrus ignored the young man and climbed the stairs to Ollette's house. Ludin had sent Sigmund and the boys away so the house was empty, though a warm fire crackled in the kitchen stove and Ollette's yippy black dog Yots greeted Arrus with a cascade of barks before scampering away to hide.

Ollette's body had been put on a table in a room just off the kitchen where people could view her before the burial. Her face was covered by a cloth, but the rest of her body sat exposed. Around the table were herbs and incense. Arrus approached Ollette, mumbling a prayer, while Johan hung back.

"What do you hope to see?" Johan asked as Arrus pulled back the cloth and put his hands on Ollette's head.

"Ollette saw the killer, so he cut out her eyes. He thought if her eyes were gone there would be no evidence."

Johan paled.

"Stupid bastard thought it was that simple," Arrus laughed.

"You take the eyes I just see what they see, wherever they are."

"Why didn't you do it in the first place?" asked Johan quickly, "we need to catch this murderer for my father."

"I was distracted, forgive me, my friend had just died," growled Arrus. "Now excuse me, I need to catch a murderer."

Arrus closed his eyes and went back through Ollette's final moment, letting Johan smell the graveyard wind, selling the lie Ludin concocted.

Johan was untouchable, free to do as he pleased. Someone who saw themselves as in that light would hold onto Ollette's eyes as a sick trophy. A smart man would've thrown them away, but Johan was invulnerable, and the invulnerable man had no need of a smart man's caution.

"What do you see?" asked Johan quickly.

Arrus waited a minute before answering, "Nothing," he growled, "It's close, but everything's fuzzy. I'll keep trying, there's no point in you waiting around for me."

Johan nodded slowly, his face ashen.

"Tonight we'll meet to dig into the other Brewmasters, I should have cracked through the veil by then," said Arrus.

"Excellent," the murderer said as he and his cronies beat a retreat back down the Malting Corridor. Arrus waited a few minutes, then ran out the back of Ollette's home and towards the Haarmann Mansion. Before he did, Arrus placed the shroud back over Ollette's head, said another quick prayer, and kissed her forehead to say goodbye.

Arrus tore through the streets, cutting into alleyways and in a few minutes he'd reached the Haarmann Mansion. Johan was still behind him but not long in coming. He tore up the street, his guards' tight goose-stepping turned into a mallard waddle as they tried to keep up. The murderer and his entourage passed through the gatehouse and Arrus went around to a postern gate Ludin had promised would be unlocked. He found the gate, turned the handle, and watched it swing open, filling him with jittery energy.

"Arrus!" Ludin hissed, and Arrus looked up to see his friend leaning out a second story window dangling a rope.

"Quick!" he said. Arrus grabbed the rope, letting himself be pulled into the mansion. Ludin was there alongside Karl and two boot squad grunts who were fidgeting nervously.

"Did he buy it?"

"Ran out the door like the house was on fire."

Ludin pumped his fist and glared at Karl triumphantly, "Lead the way."

Karl swallowed, "If you're wrong, I'm going to kill you before Frederick kills me."

Ludin pressed a knife into Karl's hand, "Slip it between the ribs if you don't mind."

"Bastard."

The junior Brewmaster led Arrus, Ludin, and the two boot squad goons through the labyrinthine mansion, past the expensive vases and varnished desks until they stood in front of a gilt door, behind which someone was ransacking the room.

Karl opened his mouth and the boot squad goons stiffened, their minds made up. They waited for the order to kick down the door, arrest Johan Haarmann, and maybe put a few boots to him, but Karl just stood, listening to Johan mutter and curse as he tore the room apart.

"Break down the damn door," snarled Arrus, shoving one of the goons who didn't hesitate and put boots to the lacquered wood, sending it flying off its hinges. In the room, Johan's guards drew blades, but their fight was short and pointless. Their comrades put them down in seconds. Johan was left cowering in the corner of his room, a glass jar clutched in his hands. The jar was filled with brown liquid, some dark beer, and a pair of eyes that turned inward, staring at him.

Arrus snatched Ollette's eyes from Johan and glared at Karl who was still dumbfounded.

"Here's your killer," spat Arrus.

"They planted those eyes!" Johan yelped, "their the killers!"

"What's going on!" screamed Frederick Haarmann, coming around the corner. He paled immediately seeing the bloody corpses and men circled around his child.

"They're the killers Father!" Johan cried, stabbing a finger at Ludin and Arrus.

"Shut up! Your son was holding this a moment ago," said Arrus holding up Ollette's eyes.

"Oh God!" the Brewmaster exclaimed, turning away.

"There are men in the boot squads helping him. Ollette saw them before she died, before your son cut out her eyes."

"Why?" hissed Frederick, stepping past Ludin and Arrus. He stood over Johan, looking down at the boy, his hands trembling.

"What did I do to deserve this from you? How did I mistreat you that you decided to wound me like this!"

"Why?" hissed Johan, "Because all your smug life I wanted you to actually suffer and know what it felt like to be looked down on and treated like an imbecile. I wanted people to look at you and see something dirty."

"This is the legacy you want to leave?"

"It's my legacy, one I forged independently, and it's yours now. You'll always be the killer's father." Johan snarled. Frederick Haarmann shook his head, motioning for the boot squads to take Johan away.

Ludin and Arrus stood silently as Frederick sagged in defeat. "Your contract will be paid by tomorrow morning. Three equal shares," the Brewmaster said before slowly walking away. Ollette's eyes following him until he disappeared around the corner.

***

The next night Cellee was in an uproar. Johan Haarmann and a ring of boot squad cronies were arrested and thrown in prison to await execution. Beer flowed for free, Frederick Haarmann's apology to the city and to the Brewmasters.

Before all that, a small group of people gathered at the edge of Cellee in a small cemetery. Ollette's service wasn't overly long and there were more laughs than tears. The burial was quick and as the last spade of earth was tamped over the coffin people began to leave. Ludin, Arrus, Sigmund, and Ollette's boys stayed. They might've stood around the grave all afternoon but Sigmund took Theo and Aldo home after three. They were worn out and with a sad smile Sigmund left Ludin and Arrus to take care of his children.

The two men stood a long time, listening to the bells remark upon the passing hours.

"We never would've caught him without her," Arrus choked out at last.

"We never caught anyone without her. I guess we're finished," he added somberly.

"A Hand and Hell-eyed man aren't much without a Hawk," said Arrus.

"No, no they're not," said Ludin, reaching into his pocket. He pulled out a drawing, a fever creation he'd finished before the funeral. It was just Ollette, Arrus, and himself sitting around the kitchen table, eating dinner and laughing. A memory he'd held onto from one of the first times they'd come together for an investigation.

He picked up a heavy rock and used it to pin the picture to Ollette's headstone. She smiled at Arrus and Ludin, her eyes twinkling with life.

The Writing on the Walls

Dawn Colclasure

Keith Harwood hated this school, but then again, he hated every school. No matter how many times his mom had assured him that "this school" would be better, he'd always had problems. Either the teachers were assholes, the students were all losers, or the coursework was too hard.

But when he looked to his mom to voice his objections about attending this school, that hopeful look on her face rendered him mute. He swallowed the lump in his throat that had been his protests and just looked to the floor. All of a sudden, the gray tiles were very interesting.

"What do you think?" his mother asked.

Keith looked ahead as they continued walking through the halls, shrugging. "It's fine."

"They have a really good reputation for sports," she said.

Keith didn't have to look at her to know she was giving him that hopeful look again. He ignored it, sighing. He had never had any interest in sports. He wished his mother would stop pushing that on him.

At least that was the only thing wrong with her. It was his dad that sent a shudder down his spine. If he wasn't on his case about spending too much time playing video games, the guy kept pushing him to get a job. Keith had filled out a couple of applications only to get his dad to shut up about it, but he really wasn't interested in delivering pizzas or flipping burgers. He sure as hell wasn't interested in brownnosing his way through a career of building skyscrapers, either. Then there was the belt his dad liked using on him or the yelling and complaining any time Keith's grades had gone down.

His mom wasn't as bad, which was why he had agreed to tour this school with her. Maybe this time he'd find better kids to hang out with here.

He noticed another rule etched on the wall in fancy script as they continued walking. It had been the first thing that caught his eye when they began walking through the school. There'd been one rule on one wall, another rule on another wall. This particular rule said, "No trash on the floors."

Keith looked ahead again. "They sure have a lot of rules."

"Rules are a good thing," his mother replied.

"I guess so," Keith allowed. "But why put them on the walls?"

"Probably a better way to remind everyone of them, I suppose."

Keith shrugged. He thought about the other rules he'd seen so far. "No smoking." "No swearing." "No sitting on the floors." "No guns or knives allowed." And then that other one about the trash. Crazy.

"Well, I like this school," his mother continued to say, as though she was just fine to continue talking even if he wasn't engaging in conversation with her. "And I think you'll like it, too." She turned to look at him. "Don't you think so?"

He shrugged. It's not like he had much say in the matter. Once she had made up her mind about something, nobody could change it. He didn't think anything he said mattered either way. She'd obviously decided to enroll him in this school. "I guess so."

***

The bell rang and Keith gathered his stuff together. He was grateful the day had finally ended. It hadn't been a good first day. All of the kids at this school sucked. If they weren't avoiding him or acting like snobs, they hardly made any conversation with him at all. He might as well have had some kind of obvious infectious disease, or something. One of those diseases with huge balls of puss all over his body. All the kids he tried to talk to took one look at him and bailed.

The teachers, at least, gave him some kind of notice. Notice enough to remind him to follow the rules "or else." There was always that "or else." What the hell did that even mean, anyway? Was he going to be thrown into solitary if he broke any of the rules?

He stood from his desk and picked up his backpack. He placed one strap over his shoulder and followed his classmates toward the exit.

"Mr. Harwood."

Keith turned to look at his teacher, Mr. Gompton, and walked over to him when he saw that his teacher had indeed called for him. He came to a stop in front of the teacher and waited.

"I noticed earlier that you tried to send some text messages in class. You probably didn't think I saw you, but I did." The teacher waited for Keith to say something and when he didn't, Mr. Gompton sighed. "Look. I know you're new here and that you're trying to fit in. But I also know why you were transferred here from Newton. We don't really tolerate students acting out very well, and it's important that you follow the rules." He leaned forward. "Just a reminder: Texting in class is against the rules." He straightened again then made sure he had Keith's attention. "Understand?"

Keith nodded. "Sorry."

Mr. Gompton nodded. "I'll let it slide this time, but consider this your warning. There won't be another one. Follow the rules, or suffer the consequences."

Keith nodded. When he was sure that Mr. Gompton didn't have anything more to say, he turned and left the classroom. As he walked through the hallway to his locker, he looked up to see one of the rules on the wall. "No smoking." He looked away, shaking his head. "Stupid rules."

He failed to see a new rule suddenly appear on a plain wall that he just walked past, "No troublemakers."

***

Keith winced as the sound of the whistle blared into his ears. He finished taking a hit from his cigarette then blew out the smoke. He dropped the butt onto the grass then smashed it out with his shoe. When he was sure that the cheerleaders were done with practice, he stood from the bleacher he'd been sitting on and walked over to the girl he'd been watching ever since he'd walked out here after school and noticed her. She had her long blonde hair up in a ponytail, long legs, and a good ass. Her tits weren't too small and she'd shown enough thin, tan body from under her cheerleading outfit. He bet if they went together, the sex with her would be great.

"Hey," he said by way of introduction as he walked up to her. He did his best smile and tried to relax.

She smiled at him. "Hey, yourself. I saw you sitting over there. What's your name?"

"Uh, Keith," he replied, nodding. He ran his hand through his brown curly hair and grinned. "What's your name?"

"Bethany," she said, smiling. "Nice to meet you."

"Same." Keith suddenly felt like it was hard to breathe. He took a few moments to get control over himself as he looked away. Was this girl a sophomore like him? Maybe it didn't matter but he tried to recall if he'd seen her in any of his classes.

"You're new here, aren't you?"

He looked at Bethany. "What?"

"At Spencer. You're new."

"Oh! You mean the school." He nodded. "Yep. First day."

"Cool."

"So," Keith muttered, clapping his hands together. "You wanna go out with me sometime?"

She smiled. "Sorry, I don't date smokers." She turned to walk away. "See ya."

Keith watched after her with disgust. Seriously? That was why she turned him down? That'd been a first. Oh, well. She was probably a lesbian anyway. "Bitch," he mumbled, walking off the field. He left the school grounds then walked home. At least this school was closer to where he lived and the better part about that arrangement is that he'd at least have some time to himself.

When he got home, he dropped his backpack onto the floor in the living room then took off his jean jacket. He threw the jacket onto the couch then walked into the kitchen. He grabbed a frozen mac and cheese meal from the freezer then put it into the microwave to cook. While he waited for his food, he walked into the living room to retrieve his cell phone and music gear from his backpack. He put the earbuds in then connected it to his phone. He tapped on his phone's screen to turn on his music then danced his way back to the kitchen. He grabbed his food from the nuke box then headed back into the living room.

After he started up his video game on the TV, Keith sat down to eat his food and play the game. After a while, he finally heard the phone ringing. He waited for it to go to voicemail but the damn thing kept ringing. Groaning, he got up from the couch and walked over to answer the phone. "Hello?"

"Good afternoon, this is Spencer High School calling about your son, Keith Harwood," an automated voice said. "Your son has broken two rules at our school today. At Spencer, we have a three strikes and you're out program set up for students who refuse to obey our rules. Your son Keith—"

"Go fuck yourself," Keith muttered, hanging up.

He walked back to the living room to continue his game but stopped when the phone started ringing again. Sighing, he walked back to answer it. He was going to have to figure out how to get the calls to go to voicemail. "Hello?"

"Good afternoon, this is Spencer High School calling about your son, Keith Harwood," the same automated voice said again. "Your son has broken two rules at our school today. At Spencer, we have a three strikes and you're out program set up for students who refuse—"

Keith hung up the phone again. "Don't care." He stood near the phone and waited. Just as he thought, it started ringing again. He picked up the receiver, disconnected the call, and then left the receiver lying on the counter by the phone. Satisfied that was the end of that, he walked back to the living room.

The phone rang again.

Keith spun around, growling. Instead of going to the phone to answer it, he marched over to unplug it instead. The phone stopped ringing. He waited and it didn't ring again.

"That's right," he muttered, nodding at the phone. "Piss off!" He marched back into the living room, hoping the rest of the game would help him forget that whole mess.

***

Lightning struck across the night sky outside of the Spencer High School building. Thunder rumbled and the rain began to fall.

Sergei Reinhold ignored the outside signs warning trespassers about prosecution as he moved inside of the school building. He poured the black paint along the hallway floor then smeared feces on the walls. He shuddered at the sight of all the words that suddenly appeared on the walls as he moved his gloved hands over them. More of those rules again. He wasn't even a student here anymore and the damn school was still tormenting him with its rules.

The building creaked from above. Sergei stopped what he was doing to look up but didn't see anything. No animals or anything up there to worry about.

He finished smearing the walls then, after removing the gloves and washing his hands, removed his flip-knife from his pocket and started carving obscene words onto the wooden walls. Next he smashed the windows that were in doors and urinated on the floors of the classrooms. He shoved mounds of toilet paper into the toilets and flushed them, staying there to make sure they all clogged up. He turned on the sinks in the restroom and left the faucets running.

As he walked through yet another hallway, he smiled. "Take that, you son of a bitch." He kicked the wall for good measure. "Stupid school! That'll teach you for expelling me!"

Sergei came to a stop as a door ahead of him creaked open. He studied it at first, thinking maybe someone was going to walk out, but nobody appeared.

He walked over to where the door stood open and looked inside. It was too dark to see anything. Lightning flashed outside and afforded him a glimpse of cleaning gear. It was obviously a janitor's closet.

"Huh. That all you got?" he chuckled, slamming the door shut.

The door swung wide open and the cleaning gear came flying out at him. A broom slammed him against the wall and held him in place as a bottle of cleaning solution sprayed into his eyes. Sergei screamed, struggling to get free. A hose snaked its way to him and moved up his body to wrap itself around his neck.

When Sergei realized what was happening, he struggled to get the hose off from around his neck. "No! Don't!"

He screamed as the hose pulled him away from the wall and down the hallway. Sergei screamed as he was dragged through the school, coming to a stop with a fierce slam against one wall. Then the hose gripped his neck even tighter and pulled him up into the air. It slammed him against two walls and spun him in a circle. The hose pulled him into the janitorial closet then strung him up on an overhead pipe. Sergei's body struggled as he hung in the air then eventually fell still.

More lightning and thunder clashed through the sky outside of the school building.

The next day, students and staff returned to the school for the day, where everything was clean, tidy and in perfect order. Nobody ever found the body of a former student hanging in the janitorial closet. Nobody saw the hole that had been made where the pipe had moved through the wall, taking the body inside of the walls with it.

***

"I'm sorry, but your son was never a student here."

Keith froze in his steps. He sidled up to the wall near the doorway and hunched against it as he listened.

"Never a student?" a woman's angry response sounded inside the office. "Of course he was a student here! At this school! That is, until you expelled him."

Silence, then she spoke again.

"I know my son was not a good boy. I know he got into trouble when he was enrolled here. But that doesn't mean you get to act like you never knew him!"

"I'm sorry. I wish I could help." Keith recognized that voice. It was the principal of the school. He hated that guy.

"You can help me! Help me find him!" the woman pleaded. "My Sergei is missing and you told the police that he wasn't even a student here!"

"That is correct," the principal said. "I even offered to share with them our records. They didn't find any evidence that your son was ever a student at this school."

"But he was!" she screamed. "You just don't care! You got rid of him and now you won't even do anything to help me find him!"

"Please, Mrs. Reinhold. Calm down. There is no need to scream. Would you care for a cup of tea?"

"No! I don't want your stupid tea! I just want to find my son!"

Before he could listen to anything else, Keith felt something pulling at his bag. He swung around with his fist flying in the air. There was a loud "crack" when his fist hit some guy's nose and the kid cried out in pain.

"Back off!" Keith warned, as the boy stumbled away from him.

"Well, well. If it isn't Mr. Harwood. Why am I not surprised."

Keith turned back around and looked up at the principal hovering over him. The principal straightened, hardening his gaze as he pointed to the doorway of the main office. "In my office. Now."

"Fuck you," Keith growled, turning to storm through the hall.

Two security guards appeared in front of him, blocking his path. Keith grumbled as he came to a stop.

"Mr. Harwood," the principal said behind him. "You will come into my office."

***

The principal stared hard at Keith. "Would you mind telling me why you struck another student?"

Keith frowned then just shrugged. He ignored the principal's bearing gaze on him and looked away, feeling bored.

The principal wasn't going to let it slide. He leaned over across his desk, looking hard at Keith as he tried to make eye contact. "I'm waiting."

Keith looked at the principal then sighed. "He touched my stuff."

"What do you mean by 'stuff'?" the principal asked, still looking straight at him.

Keith shrugged. "Just, my stuff. My bag. I was walking past him and he was trying to pull something out of it. I swung around and hit him."

The principal sat back in his seat, looking thoughtful. "I see. Are you sure he was trying to get something out of your bag?"

"Sure," Keith said, although he really wasn't. That dickhead touching his bag had no business being anywhere near him. So who cares if he was right or not? Nobody touched his stuff.

The principal folded his hands together over the desk. "We here at Spencer are aware of your behavior problems at your last school, Mr. Harwood. It would seem you have what we call a 'short temperament.' You seem to react with violence at the slightest provocation."

Keith hardened his gaze. He wasn't prepared to get all Oprah with this guy. The principal had no idea what he'd been through with bullies at school or the shit he had to deal with at home. He wasn't prepared to open up to him about it, either. "So?"

"So, that kind of behavior is not allowed at this school." He sat up, looking hard at Keith again. "We have a zero-tolerance policy for violence, Mr. Harwood. However, since you are still fairly new here and still trying to fit in, we are willing to allow you another chance. In the meantime, you are being put on temporary probation. What this means is that you will not have access to school activities, you will not be permitted to engage with students at recess, and your attendance must be perfect for a period of 10 days in a row. If, after review, we feel you have made a better adjustment to the school and its policies, we will remove you from probation, but I must warn you," here he pointed at Keith. "Another incident like this, and you will be expelled." He folded his hands together again and sat up straight, giving Keith a challenging stare. "Is that clear?"

"Crystal," Keith replied, staring hard at him. "Can I go now?"

The principal nodded. "Please see Debbie about getting a pass."

Keith got up from the chair and left the principal's office. He walked right past Debbie's desk, not even caring if his teacher was happy he had a pass or not, and left the office to return to class.

As he walked down the hallway, Keith looked at a wall and noticed one other rule written there, but this one seemed to be new; he hadn't seen it before. "No bad attitudes" it read.

Keith scoffed. "Stupid school."

He walked to the men's room and started to push open the door but the door remained locked shut and he walked right into it, bumping his head. "Ow!" he growled, rubbing the sore area. He stared at the door in confusion and tried pushing it open again. The door didn't budge.

"It's not supposed to be locked," he muttered, still staring at it.

Perhaps someone had locked it while they were in there smoking dope, or something.

Sighing, he turned to look for a janitor but didn't see one. The sound of two guys talking caught his attention and he watched as they walked into the men's room. The door swung open easily for them.

Keith scoffed again and proceeded to enter the men's room. This time, the door opened easily as he walked inside.

***

The teacher just seemed to chatter on and on. Something about boring old history. Keith struggled to stay awake. His eyelids kept falling and he kept nodding off, but then his head would jerk back up as he awoke and he tried to focus on something, anything, important.

Finally, after he'd jerked awaked for the umpteenth time, something caught his eye. "No sleeping in class" it said on the wall.

Keith stared at it. Yet another rule – or was it? He hadn't seen it there before. It's like it suddenly appeared out of nowhere.

On top of that, what kind of school had a rule like that, anyway? Of the two other schools he'd been in, not one of them had a "no sleeping in class" policy.

Just like with the "no bad attitudes" rule. Sure, school rules pretty much indicated they expected students to act right, but he didn't see that kind of specific rule at a school before.

It was like the rules he saw now were directed at him personally.

Keith scoffed as he shook his head then rubbed his eyes. Nah, that couldn't be right. He was just imagining things; that's all.

He removed his hands from his eyes and almost choked on fear when he saw a brand new rule on the classroom wall, "No imagining things."

Keith studied the words. "What the hell?" he gasped in a whisper. He looked around the classroom. The teacher was still talking as though he hadn't noticed anything. None of the kids in the class took notice of him. It's like no one else in the room had noticed the new words up on the walls.

Keith shook his head and looked down at his desk. His eyes moved to the floor and he gasped. The words this time appeared in an angry, fiery red, "No swearing."

"Hey!" he gasped, jumping up from his desk as he stepped away from it, looking at the area of the floor where the writing had appeared. He looked around and saw all of the students looking at him. He looked to the teacher and sure enough he now had the teacher's attention, too.

"Problem, Mr. Harwood?" the teacher asked, adjusting his glasses.

Keith pointed at the words on the floor. "Who did this?" he demanded.

The teacher walked over to see what Keith was pointing at. He studied the area of the floor and looked at Keith again. "Did what?"

"Who wrote that on the floor?"

The teacher balked then he assumed a more serious look as he again studied the floor. "There isn't any writing on the floor." He straightened, shrugging as he still stared. "It's just a floor."

"No, it's not!" Keith spat. He jammed his finger in the floor's direction as he spoke. "Somebody wrote 'no swearing' on the floor!"

The teacher looked up at him and smiled. "I assure you there are no words on the floor, least of all 'no swearing.'"

Keith looked at the floor. He could still see the words "No swearing." He glared at the teacher. "You're lying!"

"I am not lying," the teacher responded, bristling. He relaxed again. "Are you ill?"

Keith angrily huffed as he stared at the teacher. Was the dude blind? Did he need new glasses, or something?

"Well, then, what about that?" he asked, pointing at the two other rules that were on the wall.

The teacher turned to look in the direction that Keith pointed then turned to look at him again. "That, what?"

"That! Those words on the wall, there and there!"

The teacher followed Keith's pointing as he spoke then looked again at the other part of the wall where Keith could easily see "No sleeping in class." Finally, he turned to look at Keith again. "I'm sorry, I don't see anything."

"But I can see it!" Keith growled. He nudged a nearby student sitting at a desk. "Don't you see the words on the wall there?"

The student looked then shook his head.

"What about you?" Keith demanded of another student at her desk. She also looked then shook her head.

"What about the writing on the floor?" Keith asked her, pointing.

"Mr. Harwood, I think you should see the school nurse," the teacher interrupted. "Perhaps a nap would help."

Keith glared at him. Then he grabbed his bag from the side of his desk, the textbook he had opened on his desk, and he stormed out of the room. "Screw your nap!"

He walked through the hallway, shoving the textbook into his bag. When he looked ahead again, he noticed more rules appearing on the walls in red words. "No running." "No yelling." "No cheating on your tests." "No telling your mother you wished she was dead."

Keith groaned, rubbing his eyes as he tried to ignore the strange words appearing on the walls in such angry red lettering. Too much. This was too much. This school was too much. He had to get out of here.

"No lying," the words said on the wall now. Keith kept his eyes forward as he walked to the doors of the building.

"No sneaking out."

"No smoking pot."

"No stealing."

"No kicking small animals."

"No hitting your friends."

Keith continued walking, the hatred and anger building up within him. Those damn words. They were talking about all the bad things that he had done. Well, so what? He wasn't a saint. But he wasn't going to let whatever it was doing this to him have the upper hand, either. He wasn't going to give in to this guilt trip.

"No slashing tires." These words appeared on the walls ahead of him now, near the exit door he was walking to. Keith continued to ignore them.

"No backtalk."

"No racism."

"No shoving old ladies aside."

"No drinking."

Now the words were everywhere. They seemed to cover the walls faster and faster.

Keith hurried his steps, He was almost there. Just a couple feet away and he'd be out of this crazy evil place.

"No prank calls."

"No experimenting on animals."

"No slingshotting kittens."

"No breaking into houses."

Finally, he was at the door. Keith moved his hand up to place it on the glass window but froze as words appeared in front of him, this time in large, bold letters, "No escaping."

A loud bang behind him made Keith swing around. There was nothing and nobody there. It's like the place was entirely empty.

He turned around to try the door again when something hit him in the knee. He screamed as he dropped to the floor and grabbed his leg. He was stunned to see a hole where his knee should be. Blood oozed out of the hole.

Another boom! Keith screamed again. This time something hit his neck. He reached up to grab it and his hands came up on a pencil lodged in his neck. He heard something moving and looked up again. He recoiled in horror as he watched a large cabinet slide out of its space against the wall. It moved as though someone was pushing it. The cabinet slowly turned to face him.

"Oh, shit!" Keith gasped. He struggled to stand up and grab the doorknob. He turned his head just to see the cabinet come flying at him through the hall.

"Help!" he screamed, struggling to open the locked door.

The cabinet slammed against Keith, sending the upper half off his body out of the glass window on the door.

Keith Harwood's body hung limp on the door. The upper half and his head tore through the large, jutting glass as the cabinet behind him pulled him off of the frame. The cabinet slowly returned to its former position, dragging the boy's body with it. This time, it turned backwards so that Keith's body was towards the wall. The cabinet moved back into place, the wall behind it swallowing up the boy's body as it backed into it.

***

The ghost stood watching as students filed out of the classrooms after the bell sounded.

"Make them forget."

He did as the building had instructed him. He held his hand out over the students as they walked through the clean halls. Any sign of the recent destruction was gone; the other ghosts whose souls now belonged to the school had seen to it that the blood was cleaned up, the writing on the walls was gone, and the glass window on the door was intact.

114

Voices from the students came to him.

"Hey, I wonder where Keith went?"

"Keith" was the student he was supposed to make them all forget about. The name was somewhat familiar to him but he ignored that feeling. Now the school was his master. Now he must obey everything the school told him to do.

"Maybe he's taking a nap," the other joked, then laughed at his teacher's silly suggestion.

The first boy smiled. "Yeah, probably. Man, that guy was losing it. Talking about writing on the walls. And on the floor! I think he was seeing things."

The other nodded. "Or imagining things. Besides," he continued, looking at the plain walls and spotless hallway. "What kind of school puts writing on the walls?"

"Really," the other agreed, nodding.

The ghost sent out a wave over the students walking through the halls of the school. Forget. Forget. They would all forget the boy named "Keith Harwood." His name would be removed from the school's records. He would do as the school instructed and make sure it looked like Keith Harwood had never set foot in this school.

He moved his hand down to his side. He looked past the hall to the front door, where a mother and her teen daughter entered. This girl was not a student at the school but it looked like her mother wanted her to be. Idle chatter came to his ears about how the girl didn't want to attend this school and how her mother told her that it was either this school or juvenile hall.

Another ghost appeared closer to the floor of the hallway. He moved his hand over an area of the wall and soon the words" No swearing" appear.

The ghost now saw another ghost standing at his side. He pointed at the girl's forehead.

He looked again and saw the word appear on the girl's forehead in bold, red letters, "DEAD."

The Steel Music Box

Morgan Chalfant

Brooke Doherty gave the man a once over. He was too old to be a traditional student, but she thought he may have been a graduate student finishing up an advanced degree of some kind. He wore a white button-up shirt with the sleeves rolled just below his elbows, distressed blue jeans, and brown loafers. Around his neck was a silver crucifix dangling from a shiny silver chain. In the front pocket of his shirt was a pair of expensive aviator sunglasses and on his wrist was a paracord bracelet. She thought it strange how he was studying the lobby--like he had never seen the inside of a college dormitory before. Shrugging it off, she tapped the man on the shoulder.

"Thanks."

The man tensed, but it was a calm, collected flinch. He turned to her with a look of ignorance. His grayish eyes gleamed with a measure of uncertainty and confidence, which Brooke couldn't quite figure out. He didn't say anything. He just smiled and cast a perplexed stare.

"For holding the door, I mean," she added.

The man smiled wider. "Oh, sorry." He sighed and glanced at the elevator in front of them. "Anytime."

Brooke watched as the man walked up to the elevator and pressed the up button. Brooke bent down and stretched her legs, which had tightened up from standing still. Her run had been harder with the hot temperatures pushing ninety-five degrees.

The elevator doors slid open and the man entered with a little pep in his stride. Swiveling around, Brooke looked up to see he had stopped the doors as they started to close.

"At the risk of seeming redundant, you going up?" he said.

Brooke smirked. She usually took the stairs up for the extra physical activity, but her feet were killing her. Also, she was wiped. The heat had sapped her reserves. Just this once, she thought. She nodded and stepped into the elevator. Leaning up against the left wall, she grasped the aluminum railing as the elevator doors slammed shut. She sighed, knowing she was trapped with the horrible elevator music for seven floors.

"Floor?" the man asked.

"Eight. Top floor."

The man pushed eight. Brooke waited to see what button the man pressed for himself, but he just stepped back and let the old elevator do its work.

"You going to eight too, huh?" she said.

He nodded with a faint smile.

The elevator groaned and began humming upward. The usual sounds of stretching steel and unoiled cables resounded through the metal box. The dormitory was at least thirty years old, which made the elevator twice that from constant use. At least that's how she figured it. Regardless, it was exactly why Brooke never took the elevator; this one or any other.

She took a deep breath and leaned back against the wall on her side. She had already begun to regret her decision. If she had just huffed it up the stairs, she would probably already be in her dorm room and well on her way to a nice warm shower. As her decisions went, this was definitely not one of her better ones.

The man stood across from her, checking his watch. The normal cacophony continued from the speakers overhead. "Girl from Ipanema." Screaming seemed like a good idea. Elevator music. Adding misery to transportation since--well, whenever the elevator had been invented. She didn't know. Nevertheless, the endless droning was pure torture. The elevator was one miserable steel music box. That was all.

Suddenly, she heard the barely audible hum coming from the stranger. He was giving her a playful smirk, peering at her out of the corner of his eye.

"Don't start." She smiled.

The man nodded and ceased his teasing. He checked his watch again. Brooke tried to catch a glimpse of the time as well. No luck. She couldn't see what brand it was either, but being a girl who was slightly materialistic, which she wasn't afraid to admit, she knew accessories and could tell the watch was expensive. When the man finally looked up, she smiled.

"What time is it?"

The numbered lights above the doorframe lit up one by one, steadily making the journey from left to right. The Weist Hall elevator had always been miserably slow. Two. Three. Four. Then, when the fifth floor light sprang to life, the elevator jolted to a harsh stop. Brooke found herself letting out a quick shriek. Groaning metal echoed through the elevator. Brooke white-knuckled the railing. She swore she heard cables tearing. The elevator shook for a moment and then stopped. When she regained her bearings, she saw the man didn't seem fazed. He simply cast peevish glances to the corners of the elevator and sighed.

"Apparently it's time they fixed the elevator," he said. "Shoddy maintenance, don't you think?"

He tilted his head down and looked at her. Brooke felt like the man was undressing her with his eyes. He didn't seem frightened, just annoyed. Something was there she hadn't noticed before, but she couldn't put her finger on it. Who wasn't freaked out about being stuck in an elevator? Her chest heaved and her breathing was rampant. She clutched the railing tighter. The one time she decided to take the easy way up and this happens. Murphy's Law. They could just as easily change the name to Brooke's Law.

"Relax," the man said. "Calm down."

"Calm down?" Brooke glared at him. "That's the one thing you're not supposed to say to someone who's panicking."

"My mistake," he replied. "But you're way past panicking."

"We're stuck in an elevator!" Brooke exclaimed. "Of course I am!"

"Don't suppose you have a cell phone on you?" The man eyed her up and down. The tight green spandex athletic top clung to her sweat soaked frame like a second skin and the tiny black shorts left no room to carry anything. "I suppose not."

"Good guess." She exhaled and finally let go of the railing. "You?"

The man shook his head. "No."

"Well, that's just great."

"Never would have guessed a girl your age would be without her cell for five minutes," he replied.

"I've got a lot on my mind." She replied. "I forgot it when I went to run."

"Well, we aren't running away from this problem."

Brooke slid down the wall and sat in one of the corners of the elevator, running her hands through her damp hair. The man eased down onto the floor as well in the adjacent corner near the door.

"You don't seem worried at all," Brooke said. "It's kinda annoying."

Brooke watched a grin widen on the man's face and disappear.

"Annoyed is what I am. I have an appointment to get to.... Don't worry, sure someone'll come along and figure out the elevator's broken ...

sooner or later." He checked his watch again. "Nothing we can do but wait."

"What's your name?" he asked smoothly, scratching an itch on his cheek. "If you don't mind me asking."

Brooke looked at the stranger in silence. The way he spoke was eloquent. Almost charming. The first thing she noticed was his perfect teeth. The glassy neutral grey of his eyes ran a close second. They seemed to dissect anything they fell upon. Predatory, but strangely, she did not find his stare unpleasant. Of course, she was just happy to not be alone in the elevator.

The distance he kept between them added some comfort as well, as though he didn't wish to startle her. He probably worked a high pressure job, Brooke thought, one where he had to deal with all sorts of stressful situations just like their current one. It's the only thing she could think of at the moment that would explain his steel demeanor. Yes, at least she wasn't alone. That would have been worse.

"Brooke." She extended her hand.

The man nodded. "Graysen." He rocked forward onto his knees and stretched across the expanse between them, extending his hand. "Max Graysen. Call me Max."

Brooke reached out and shook the hand. His palms were warm, but not moist or clammy like she thought they would be. His grip was firm, but not uncomfortable. His eyes fell to her polished red nails, then he returned to his place in the corner.

"Nice nails," he commented. "Red's a good color on you."

Brooke didn't know to respond. It was slightly creepy being complimented by a perfect stranger, but at the same time, compliments were compliments. It was a friendly enough gesture. She figured Max for trying to keep her mind off their predicament.

Finally, she gave him an appreciative nod and said, "Thank you."

"So, Brooke, what's a girl like you doing in a place like this?"

A laugh escaped her lips before Brooke could even think. Now, it was painfully obvious he was trying to distract her from the situation. He really was a silver-tongued devil. She figured she could humor him. Anything was better than dwelling on their unpleasant circumstances.

"I'm horrible, I know," he said. "My friends always joked that I was a bit crazy. Used to call me Mad Max."

"Nice .... No, no, I needed that. Thanks." Brook licked her dry lips.

"So, what's your major?" he asked. "You got a ... I wanna say sociology, maybe psych, look to you."

"Not bad." She nodded and smiled. "Psychology."

"Just psych? Any particular emphasis?" Max asked, fixing a flaw in his left rolled sleeve.

"Well, Criminal Psych, but I'm not quite sure. I may change it."

Max nodded his head. "That wouldn't be the first change either, would it?"

Brooke's eyes became thin slits. She was taken off guard how well the stranger had read her. She brushed a strand of hair out of her eyes and replied, "What makes you say that?"

Shrugging, Max replied, "Just good at reading people. You seem like someone who hasn't quite found her niche. You're running on a night when most would be studying. Finals week, right--which means you either care about your body or have a lot on your mind and needed to clear your head."

"Nice. That's pretty good," she replied. "So you mentioned an appointment. What are you, a tutor or something?"

"Or something."

"What's that supposed to mean?"

Max tilted his head and said, "What do you think it means?"

"So if you're not a tutor, then what? I was gonna go with graduate student, but now ... I doubt it."

"Why?"

Brooke shrugged. "I don't know."

Brooke observed Max as he nodded and fished into the hip pocket of his jeans and pulled out a packet of gum. He pulled a stick out for himself and offered some to her. She took a piece. She wasn't normally a gum chewer, but maybe chewing something would ease the tension and make time pass quicker. She hoped.

"So, why couldn't I be a grad student?" Max inquired, standing up. "I'm curious."

"Oh, you are? Sorry, I didn't think--"

"No, I'm not. I'm just asking you why you think I couldn't be."

Brooke swallowed, nearly losing her gum. Max's conversational skills hads swiftly begun to change. Even his posture had gone from perfect with straight and shoulders back to casual and calculating. His expressions were analytical, like he was studying her, almost as if she was a puzzle that needed to be solved.

"Uh, I really don't know. You seem way too mature. Worldly, I guess. Learned."

"Guess you could say that."

121

"So what is it you do then?" Brooke asked. "Don't tell me your son is here something. That'd be a strange story to tell. 'Hey, I was just trapped in an elevator with your dad!'"

"Stranger things have happened." He chewed his gum loudly for a moment.

Brooke watched him fingering the paracord bracelet. He began to laugh. She found herself becoming a little unnerved. Max's laugh was strange. It wasn't content or one of humor. The tone was weird, like he was amused, but his mind was somewhere else. Distant. There was a carefree indifference to the way it left his mouth. She'd never heard a laugh like that.

He finally lifted his eyes and said, "And hardly, I've killed too many sons to have any of my own."

Brooke laughed, thinking she had heard him wrong. "Excuse me."

He tilted his eyes to the ceiling as if in deep thought and said, "Quite a few daughters too."

Brooke gulped. "What? What do you mean?" She slid herself casually into the corner furthest from him.

"Exactly what I said," he replied, checking his watch again. "Hard to believe it's been half an hour already. Getting a little stuffy in here." He looked right through her. "Cramped. Don't you think?"

Brooke tried to keep herself calm and collected. Max was just speaking figuratively, she told herself. She looked at him again. From his height and build and the way his short dark hair was cut, he was probably in the military. That was it. He was probably back home on leave or had been discharged and was having trouble dealing with the things he saw over there. PTSD. That was it. Or she had completely misconstrued what he was saying.

The half-silence was palpable. The elevator music groaned through the speaker overhead. It was as monotonous as her situation, Brooke thought. She stared across at Max off and on for several minutes. She studied him. His mannerisms and movements. The way he scratched an itch above his eyebrow. The fact he picked at his teeth with a toothpick he pulled from his pocket. The sporadic checking of his watch.

Finally, Max broke the hush that had fallen over the elevator.

"Not polite to stare, Brooke."

"I--I'm sorry. I just--"

"Go ahead. Ask me. It's perfectly alright. Ask me what you've been dying to ask me for the last six minutes."

She swallowed. "You serious? About killing?" she asked, a tremor in her voice. "You're in the military aren't you, that's what you meant, huh?"

Max scoffed. "Now Brooke, do I really look like someone who takes orders?" He cleared his throat. "That's not the question. I know you're thinking it, might as well get it out in the open. Off your chest." He chuckled, waving his hands about. "We're not going anywhere."

Brooke paused. She knew the question. The one bouncing around in her brain. The one she hoped wasn't true and was just paranoia stemming from the stressful situation. What were the odds? There was no way a thing like this could happen, she thought. But then she considered that's what all victims probably thought.

Max snapped his fingers, bringing her out of her thinking trance.

"Come on, you know you want to." Max smiled. "What's the worst that could happen?"

Brooke curled her sweaty palms into fists and spoke.

"Are you...a killer?" she asked. "Like a serial killer?"

Max leaned toward her and whispered, "Yes."

Brooke's eyes went wide in shock, even though she had known what the answer was. There was still plenty of space between them, but Brooke felt like she could feel Max's breath on her skin. He may as well have been crushing her into the corner of the elevator. She was trapped. She was trapped in a steel box with a murderer five floors up over nothing but air. And the music droned on, compounding her mental breakdown. Her nerves were becoming more fried by the second.

"I really don't like titles, especially that one ... but yes," he said.

She turned to the small plastic bulb in the top corner to the right of the elevator door. It was the security camera the university had installed because people were having sex in the elevator. All it had done was increase students' daring. In her fear, Brooke had forgotten it was even there.

Max made no move to stop her. She expected him to, but he didn't. He just stood calmly leaning in the corner opposite her as she frantically waved her arms and screamed for help. Brooke banged on the doors and shouted at the top of her lungs.

"We both know that thing isn't on," Max said. "You really think I'd let myself be caught on camera?" He shook his head. "I've been doing this for quite some time. Only an amateur would make that mistake."

Brooke quit waved her arms and stopped yelling. She knew that too. The thing was always malfunctioning--that, or the person at the front desk was never watching it. The resident assistants didn't get paid enough to waste their time with their eyes locked on the screen. Either way, she was totally screwed. She hadn't counted on Max knowing anything about Weist. Apparently, he had done his research. She was right. He was learned.

Brooke's panic changed to anger. "Speaking of mistakes, what do you call getting yourself stuck in a steel cage?"

Max laughed. "A complication. Nothing that can't be remedied."

Brooke stepped back into the corner, putting her hands out in front of her. Beads of sweat collected on her forehead. A chill passed up her spine, despite it be overly warm in the elevator. It was a shiver like no other she had ever felt before. One of living fear and growing despair.

"So, you're gonna ... you're gonna kill me."

She gulped and watched him reach into his jean pocket again. He was going for his weapon. A knife. A piece of wire. Some strange killing instrument she'd never heard of. Balling her fists, Brooke prepared for him to attack. Her nerves were shot. Adrenaline began pumping. Her breathing became rampant. Then, Max revealed a tube of chapstick.

"Why would I?" he asked, popping the cap off and rubbing the chaptick across his top and bottom lip.

"I suppose if you were, you wouldn't tell me anyway, huh?"

She watched him return the tube to his pocket and slide his lips together then take his finger and run it out around his lips, wiping off any stray balm.

"Course I would," he replied. "You've been so honest. Least I can do is offer the same."

Suddenly, Brooke heard voices echoing up the elevator shaft. She could barely make them out, but the voice was telling them to hold on for a little longer and that they were working on getting the elevator going again. Max clearly heard them too.

"Well, that was quick," Max said.

Brooke moved as close to the doors as possible and began shouting again. She pounded on the door with closed fists, bruising her delicate hands.

"That's really not going to help," Max said nonchalantly. "I mean I could have killed you a dozen times already. I could right now and those technicians down there couldn't do a thing about it. I'd be gone before they got us moving again."

Brooke spun around and put her back to the door. "Yeah ... but if you do, they'd catch you. There'd be no doubt you were the one who did it."

"Maybe." He flashed her the same razor blade smile. "I could make it look like an accident too. This isn't my first dance, Brooke. That's assuming I was still here." Max pointed to the maintenance hatch above them.

"It's sealed!" Brooke shouted.

"Is it?"

Max pushed off the railing and stood straight up. Using the railing, he bridged himself up, pushed open the hatch, and then dropped back down to the floor. He had thought of everything.

Fear gripped Brooke like never before. It felt like Death was grabbing hold of her spine. She couldn't breathe. Max stood there smiling at her, staring through her with those steely grey eyes of his, lips parted in an insidious grin.

"Bet you wish you took the stairs now, huh."

The stark living terror that enveloped Brooke was too much for her to bear. She hadn't had a panic attack since she was in junior high. She felt it coming on, though. It ambushed her. Collapsing on the floor, her chest felt tight, she shook like a palsy patient, and darkness flooded her vision.

**

When Brooke awoke, she was lying in the back of an ambulance. A paramedic was checking her vital signs. The ambulance was parked in the front parking lot of Weist, she could tell since the back doors were open. Outside, two firemen were climbing back into their truck and a few gawking students milled around trying to catch a peek inside the ambulance.

"You're gonna be fine, hun," the paramedic, a middle-aged Latino woman, said with a smile. "We just need to take you on up to the hospital to check you out. You took a nice shot to the head. Just relax. You're safe."

Brooke nodded. She was still a little groggy. "Where's the guy that was trapped with me?"

"Guy? It was just you, hun. Being alone in there really musta freaked you out, but you're okay. From the looks of it, you fainted and hit your head on the railing inside the elevator. There was a bit of blood, but nothing too serious. I'm gonna get my kit outside and then we're off to the hospital, okay?"

She sighed and tried to insist she was not alone, but the paramedic wouldn't listen to her, assuring her everything was going to be okay. The woman covered her with a blanket and stepped out of the ambulance.

Brooke shifted on the gurney. Her head ached. She felt a lump just above the temple. Suddenly, as she shifted again, something sharp jabbed her inside her top. Fishing down inside, mashed between her breasts, was a small folded piece of paper. She opened it and read.

Brooke,

You passed out before I had a chance to say goodbye. It was lovely chatting with you. Not every day I get to be that honest with someone. It was quite liberating. Thank you. If I were you, I'd stick with Criminal Psych. Our little conversation would make one helluva paper topic, don't you think? After all, it's not every day someone gets to have a candid talk with someone like me ... and live to tell the tale. I'll say hi to your roommate for you. Good luck with finals.

Kind regards,
Max

Brooke's eyes widened. Her heart raced again. All she could do was scream as the ambulance doors closed.

To the End of the Dream

John Kaniecki

"Her face, tell me what her face looked like," Doctor Mumbakata cried out in over flowing excitement, "what does her face look like?"

There was a pause and then a voice speaking in a meek whimper, "I don't know; I looked away."

"By the seven angels of the seven seas," surged the angry voice of the psychiatrist, "you will never reach recovery until there is conclusion. You must face your fears, your must see what is beyond the black veil."

"But the face is hideous," said Walter Winimore, "I'm frightened."

"See there," said the good Doctor calming down from his surge of adrenalin, "how by any logical means can you determine the appearance of the woman if you do not first view her features?"

"But the voices they tell me-"

"Ah the voices again," Mumbakata said scornfully, "they are nothing more than your inhibitions getting in the way of your progress."

Walter Winimore felt the dampness under his arms caused by his perspiration. His deodorant had kicked in filling the small office with a sweet cinnamon aroma. Across at his desk sat a large man. In fact Doctor Mumbakata could be considered a giant. He not only stood a tall seven feet but filled in his designer suit with broad muscles. The man's hands and face were dark brown. His hair immaculately trimmed. Upon his broad nose sat glasses with a black frame and thick lenses. His face was one full of utter disgust. One could imagine that the doctor was a father just hearing his teenage daughter was pregnant.

"The voices, they are angels trying to protect me from-" Winimore again could not complete his thought.

"From whom?" roared the ogre, "what is her name?"

"Ah, please," cried out Walter, "have some mercy upon me, I'm trying the best that I can."

The psychiatrist reclined in his chair. His disturbed face went blank as if he was the perfect practitioner of high stakes poker. In his hand he tapped his pen several times upon the small notebook he was holding. "Mercy?" Doctor Mumbakata said, "did you say mercy?"

"Yes doctor," called out the patient, "you're pushing me to hard!"

"Really," said the large man his Haitian accent coming out to the surface, "and what about it?" The doctor sat and let a good measure of time slip by in silence. "Here I am, Walter, treating you, and free of charge none the less. Do you not appreciate that? Or do you feel entitled?"

"Ah come on, Doc," squealed Walter.

"Come on," repeated the psychiatrist, "are we going to take a journey?" The words were spoken without any effort to hide the sarcasm. "I believe the only place that you are going is back into the psychiatric hospital."

"Oh please, Doctor, I'll do anything, please don't send me back there."

"Will you really, Walter Winimore, will you really?" the Doctor was now tapping his pen swiftly. As if a drummer heading to a climax of a song.

"I swear it, you don't know what it's like in there," Winimore said full of anxiety.

"Yes, I have an idea or two," said the Doctor with a jovial laugh. "Not a pleasant place sometimes is it? Especially in the committed ward, unit three b."

"Oh God have mercy," cried Walter Winimore, "I was almost beaten to death there and raped and the staff are Satanists."

"Do you know I could have you committed just for expressing delusional thoughts as you are exhibiting right now?" Doctor Mumbakata wore a triumphant grin over his face exposing his pearly white teeth.

Walter Winimore sat in his chair and started to tremble in terror.

"Come now, Walter," said the psychiatrist, "let us reason together." Again the doctor allowed silence to creep into the flow of the conversation. "I am here to help you am I not?"

"Yes," said Walter, "I know that."

"You do trust me don't you?"

Now it was Walter's time to allow the silence to pass.

Irritated after several swift seconds the doctor snapped, "We are five minutes over in our session Mister Winimore and I have other clients to see, paying clients mind you."

"Well thanks," said Walter contritely.

"You are most welcome," said Doctor Mumbakata in a jovial tone, "you shall schedule an appointment with my secretary Doris in one week time."

Walter Winimore rose quickly from his seat and hastily headed towards the door. "And one more thing," called out the shrink.

Walter froze dead in his tracts. "Yes, Doctor," he croaked out meekly.

"Have a nice day," said the psychiatrist softly.

Walter opened the door hustling through and then quickly closed it behind him. The good doctor sat in his chair placing the note book and pen upon his cluttered desk. He then picked up a wooden carving of a woman's face that sat adjacent to his computer screen. It was an African woman that was hand carved. Mumbakata attained it when he was traveling in Egypt. He was walking the curving narrow back streets of Cairo when he happened upon it. The wooden bust was sitting in a open window. When Mumbakata saw it he heard it sweetly call out his name. He could not resist the seductive beckoning. The psychiatrist's life had never been the same since it became his possession. The owner didn't want to part with his precious treasure. However two massive hands snapping his neck did a rather convincing job in relinquishing the prize.

"Ah, Mother Nefertiti," said Mumbakata picking up the wooden statue, "I am getting nowhere with this cretin."

The wooden statue hissed and spit out a forked tongue like a snake. "You are being far too easy on him," scolded the statue.

"I threatened to have him committed to unit three B," said the Doctor in defense, "that is his worst fear."

"Nay," spoke the wooden head, "his worse fear is to look upon her face."

"If I push him too fast he will break," cried out the Doctor. Mumbakata knew that he had displeased his Mistress. The human was well aware of the pain the she could inflict if it was her desire. "I am a trained clinician, experienced in the field of mental health. I have been licensed for over twenty years and I have written three text books on the matter and taught at the University."

"Yes, that is all true," said Nefertiti, "but you are now talking to a block of wood."

In anger the good doctor slammed the bust on his desk. His mind reeled in worrisome thought. What do psychiatrists do when they go crazy?

"Hey, Walter," beckoned the man from the open car window. "Wanna go for a ride?"

"Not today, Harold," called out Winimore.

"Oh come on, Walter," the sun glass wearing occupant of the passenger seat cried, "or are you going to make my life hard?"

"Look, I got a lot on my mind," said Walter as he turned to head into a store boldly turning his back to the pair in the Mercedes.

"I got some of this sugar," sung Harold sweetly.

Walter turned his head backwards to see the man dangling a package. It was a clear plastic bag inside it was a yellowish powder. "No thanks," cried Winimore resisting the overwhelming urge, "I remember what happened last time you gave me a present."

"Look, Walter, we gotta talk," Harold said now yelling seething mad, "we're gonna talk, one way or the other." The man in the car lifted a black gun flashing it and then quickly retrieved it.

"Nice try, Harry," called out Walter, "much too crowded for you to play around with toys like that today isn't it?"

The Mercedes Benz's tires squealed and there flew up a cloud of dust and smoke. Walter could smell the scent of burnt rubber. The middle aged man coughed. Damn he thought, what does the Company want with him now? Walter continued down the street hustling with all urgency. The side street he was on had a good number of people. Immediately paranoia set in. Of the fifty people in sight how many were CIA agents trying to abduct him? Walter did his best to calm himself down. No way all of these people could be out to get him. Not that the Agency was lacking in any resources. It was just that Walter wasn't that important a person for an all out abduction operation.

By instinct Walter walked down two stores to a clothing store. Then he proceeded passing through the racks of apparel to the back of the store. The clerks and cashiers stared at the middle aged man rudely gawking. Winimore was disheveled in appearance. His face hadn't been shaved this week so he sported a fledgling mustache and beard. He was wearing a gray jacket which was both tattered and smudged with dirt. Upon his head was a brown hat. Walter walked to the back of the store. He then promptly exited out of a door with a sign saying 'fire exit' above it.

"Hey, that's only for emergencies!" screamed a store associate at the top of his lungs.

Walter took off his hat and waved it to the offended employee. "I'm in a hurry!" he cried out. Walter emerged into a narrow back alley. On either side were various trash dumpsters. The middle aged man needed to make a quick decision on whether to go left or right. There were no other options to him then to hide or break into another store. While the latter would most likely keep him out of the hands of the Company people it would wind him up in jail. Hiding was only a temporary solution. Again following instinct Walter took a left.

In a hurried pace the man shuffled in his worn out shoes to the edge of the alley. He was almost running. At the end was a major avenue in the city and it would have hundreds of people on it. The CIA was bold and often brazen, but New York had hosts of security cameras. Of course the Company had no fear of the police, but Walter knew there were other organizations in this world. The man had just reached the end of the alley when the black Mercedes Benz pulled up. Harold was sitting there with his gun drawn out. "Get in now or I'll kill you," the armed man snarled.

Walter seeing no viable options wasn't willing to see if this was a bluff. Meekly like a whipped dog Winimore obliged Harold's command. With utter gloom the man opened the car door and got inside. He slinked to the back of the leather seat wishing he could disappear.

A large man with muscles bulging out of his gray pinstripe suit in the driver's seat spoke. "Ain't ya glad to see me, Wally?"

"Why, of course," said Walter in a whisper, "it's always good to see you, Bert."

"Hey, Wally," said the beast as he pressed his massive foot on the gas pedal causing the car to lunge forward.

"Yes, Bert," said Winimore meekly wanting to disappear into nothing.

"I'm gonna bust your face up real good for messing with us," said the agent in vitriol anger.

"Please, Bert, have a little mercy on a guy down on his luck."

"You know the rules, Wally, we gotta set an example."

Walter Winimore looked for some way of escape. It was going to be a very bad day.

***

"Doctor Mumbakata!" cried out the nurse, "hurry this way."

The psychiatrist hurried with his black satchel in his hand. The attendant led him into a room. There lay Walter Winimore upon a bed.

His face was unrecognizable. The nose was blown up three sizes too large. Both eyes were blackened. His left arm was in a white cast as was his suspended right leg. "By the Fates," cried out Doctor Mumbakata upon seeing his patient. "Is he conscious?" he asked.

"I hear ya loud and clear, Doc," said wounded man. "Loud and clear," he repeated.

"Good Lord, Walter," called out the Doctor, "what happened to you?" The Doctor paused. "Who did this to you?"

"Ah," said Walter, "I'd better not say."

"Well," interjected the nurse, "when Mister Winimore was admitted we did a blood test."

"What were the results?" the Doctor inquired.

"He almost over dosed on heroin."

"Ah ,Walter," cried the psychiatrist, "I am truly disappointed in you." As was his pattern the psychiatrist let the weight of his words sink in. "I gave you my private number just in case of temptation."

"It ain't like that, doc," cried out Walter, "I can explain."

"Nurse," called out Mumbakata as a captain of the army ordering his troops. "What this man needs is a good sleep, get some sedatives."

Walter began to shake. "Come on, Doc," he cried out, "you know what happens when I fall asleep."

The nurse retreated out of the room on her mission. "Indeed I do, Walter," said they psychiatrist softly. "And this time we are going to the end of the dream."

Walter began to sweat and shake nervously. He was in a true panic. Of all the things in the world he feared most was to look upon the face of the strange woman. "Please, Doctor Mumbakata," the wounded man pleaded, "anything but that."

The nurse returned looking quite agitated. Without saying a word she attended to the intravenous solution. The white clad lady took out a needle and injected a liquid into the apparatus. A clear liquid filled the top of the tube. "I've done as you requested," reported the nurse.

"Thank you," said the psychiatrist. "And please don't have anybody disturb us," the good doctor said softly, "we'll be having therapy."

"I understand completely," said the nurse as she departed closing the door behind her.

"And that just leaves you, me, and Nefertiti," said brown ogre tapping his black satchel.

***

"So you're saying that there is no way that the man knows that there is a camera in that room?"

A.J. the hospital's head of security gave off an audible sigh of frustration. Asking such a naive question proved that this man was without a doubt not an FBI agent. The security chief had not only validated the I.D., but he also called the New York office of the g-men. On both counts the test was passed. A.J. was extremely concerned over privacy issues. Without a warrant what they were doing was highly illegal, but still more perplexing was the reason why. For all the security chief could surmise is that some junkie couldn't pay for his high and he was made an example to other debtors.

"And there's no way to hear what they are saying?" asked the man in the suit.

A.J.'s face got a perplexed look. "As I stated before there is no audio in any of our camera systems for our entire security net, only visual."

"Is there any way you could get audio?" queried the alleged g-man.

"Well you might try putting your ear to the door," shot A.J. sarcastically.

"Great idea," cried the stranger. "Hey, what's he doing now?"

If A.J. didn't see it with his own eyes he wouldn't have believed it. "Well he's taking out a small wooden statue of some sorts from his bag."

"If there any way to zoom in?"

"Unfortunately, no," said the security chief, his interest now rising astronomically.

***

Doctor Mumbakata was convinced William Winimore was sleeping. The bust of Nefertiti was sitting upon the desk next to the bed the badly beaten man was lying on. The psychiatrist thanked the Fates for such an opportunity as this to arise. Surely this was a sign that they were favorable to his desires. More importantly, to the desires of his grand Mistress.

The dark giant took out a needle from his bag. "May your blessing be upon it, oh Wonders of the Heaven," he recited as he injected the sleeping William with the potion. What a great thing to combine the dark arts with science. Mumbakata thought about his upbringing in Haiti. He saw many things that science could never explain. Men walking on hot coals with no damage to their feet. People being struck with illnesses suffering from the identical symptoms as depicted by a voodoo priest. He did not dabble in that arcane religion, but he believed it had merit. It was not until Cairo where he met his savior that he turned to the darkness.

The injection was a substance that weakened the will. It would bring the victim to a state of willing compliance to almost any action. In his brief stint in the United States Army, Doctor Mumbakata had been involved with experimentation on individuals. In particular the impoverished citizens of Haiti. While outside of the racial barriers and culture of the hierarchy of the armed forces Mumbakata's skills were invaluable. He alone could converse in the native language of the human guinea pigs. This was key to the success of the experimentation.

"How are you feeling?" asked the Doctor.

William stirred in his bed unable to move. "I am in pain."

"The pain is passing," encouraged Mumbakata, "the drugs have taken away all of the pain."

"I feel no pain," said Winimore. A wisp of a smile came to the surface of his face.

"You are entering your dream," said Mumbakata softly.

"Ah I am walking down an alley," said Walter.

"Is it day or night?" asked the psychiatrist.

"It is night," replied the patient in his semiconscious state.

"How do you see then?" asked the Doctor.

"The stars are shining brightly," answered Walter.

"So you can see things clearly?"

"Yes, the stars are bright the path is clear," said the dreamer.

"Excellent, you are feeling better, much better," said Doctor Mumbakata. He knew he had to handle this extremely slow. He would not get another chance like this. In fact he was not certain how the truth serum would interact with the other chemicals that were in Walter Winimore's system. The Doctor knew that many of their test subjects perished with just being injected with the potion alone, but the psychiatrist had refined the solution diluting it to diminish toxic effects. Of course Mumbakata had evoked the blessing of his Mother Mistress and that emboldened him to a feeling that he would be successful.

"I am walking down the alley and I see somebody," Walter spoke.

Doctor Mumbakata smiled grandly and let out a tremendous sigh of relief. He knew from his extensive experience that he had the patient exactly in the proper state of mind. The key was that the subject would reveal what was going on his mind without having to be prompted. Of course a clever interrogator could help subtly navigate the slipstream of the subconscious. The dark giant was confident of success, now more than ever. "Thank you, Mother Mistress," he prayed bowing his head to the likeness of the African queen. The wooden statue winked her eye and smile briefly before returning to a cold inanimate state.

"I see a woman," Winimore called out.

Doctor Mumbakata sat up and listened intently. His interest was piqued. The woman was the key. In her identity hung perhaps the whole fate of the Earth. The psychiatrist waited for Walter to reveal more of the vision he was experiencing in his slumbering mind. No words came forth. A good anxious minute passed. Things were not working according to plans. The patient at this stage should be chattering with no interruptions. The physician decided he needed to intervene. "What is happening, Walter?"

"I am walking down the alley,"

"Good," encouraged the giant man, "go on."

"She is dressed in black garments as if she is in mourning. There is a veil covering her face."

Doctor Mumbakata felt a great sense of self satisfaction. He was nearing the end of the quest which began fifteen years ago in Cairo when he first met his Mother Mistress. The doctor had snapped the elderly man's neck who coveted his idol. It was a baptism of evil. Though Mumbakata was formerly a captain in the United States army he had never killed or even seriously harmed anybody. To brutally murder somebody, especially with bare hands, forever changes a human psyche. A killer walks through a forbidden door to a barren realm that should not exist. Mumbakata had sold his soul, not to the devil, but to his own personal deity.

Nefertiti would commune with the doctor in times of secret passions of solitude. She spoke in hushed whispers to her servant, Mumbakata of the golden age of Africa. She was a goddess, the very essence of fertility. The Egyptian queen was brown seduction in sweetest purity. Africa was the birth place of life. The Dark Continent was the motherland of all humanity. Nefertiti was the queen of Kush. Mumbakata by way of Haiti was a stolen son, but still in every way family. In fact the Doctor was the chosen vessel. The torch had been passed and Mumbakata was chosen to be the bearer of the flame, her Lucifer.

The Mother Mistress lurked in an ether domain. Presently her powers were limited to the shadows. In all the vast realm of the living she could only touch one individual. In her true home, the dark nether land her powers waxed strong. According to the stars the time was coming soon for the unleashing of another age. The exact details Nefertiti could not as yet comprehend nor discern. However she did possess dark arcane knowledge. She knew that the new age would soon be ushered in by a woman. To know the identity of that woman was key for any gambit for power. And thus, Walter Winimore.

***

"Okay," said A.J. staring at the black and white screen with almost no action occurring, "level with me."

"Huh," said the man in the suit. He was so intensely staring at the screen that he refused even to turn towards the security chief when he was asked a question.

"I mean what's going on here?" inquired the captain of the hospital guard.

"I explained it all to you," said the alleged federal agent in a dismissive tone as if he was annoyed at the disturbance.

"Okay," said A.J. getting angry, "I can cut this all down with the flick of one switch."

The man looked up and stared at A.J. His face was flushed red with furry. "You wouldn't dare interfere with the investigation of the Federal Government! You're nothing but a two bit punk security guard. Learn your lesson well." The man turned back to focus all his attention on the screen.

A.J. sat silent allowing his mind to harness calm. Being an officer in the Green Berets had taught him discipline among many other important life lessons. "No warrant, no screen," said A.J. in defiant determination. He extended his left hand and flicked of the screen.

"Turn it on right now," growled the man in the suit.

A.J. looked at him with a smile. He saw that the man's right hand's fingers were forming to deliver a blow. The security guard knew that is would be a blow to the neck. The man moved swiftly. In fact quicker then A.J. had anticipated, but the security chief was at one time a world class competitor of martial arts. He had fought in Japan, Korea and China with the best of the best. To him this man was just a palooka with a glass jaw. The thrust came from the foe. A.J. took his left hand and directed the force of the attack past him. Simultaneously his right hand grabbed the attacker and pulled him forward. The alleged g-man lunged forward and fell promptly on the floor with A.J. securely on top of him. A.J. twisted the man's arms in a lock that was extremely painful. "There are many lessons in life," said the ex Green Beret, his pride salvaged.

"Get the hell off of me now," ordered the man in a muffled cry.

"Learn some respect first," said A.J. defiantly. He twisted the wrist of the man ever so slightly. This was accompanied with an outburst of agony.

"Damn you," cried the man, loud as he could.

"Look, I don't know who you are and I don't know what you want. But I do know that you are certainly not an F.B.I. agent. I'll wager to bet that you had my phone call to the agency's headquarters rerouted to some other office."

"Pure speculation," cried the man.

"Perhaps," said A.J. "But with minimal effort I could haul you and your I.D. down to F.B.I. head quarters down town and have them take a scrutinizing look at your credentials."

The man surged in anger but then calmed down rapidly as if he was a rat looking for a way out of a maze and then coming to the understanding it was all a hoax with no way out. "Okay, okay, what do you want?"

"You're name would be a good start, and your real name please."

"I'm Harold, and please for god's sake let me up. It is very important that I see what is happening in that room. For the love of god."

A.J. smiled. He now had the upper hand, at least for the moment.

***

Once tasting the sweet surge of seductive pleasure from Nefertiti, Doctor Mumbakata served her with an unmatched zeal. The psychiatrist was well on his way to a stellar and extremely lucrative practice in the New Jersey suburbs in the shadow of the skyscrapers of Manhattan. However his dark Mistress had identified New York City as the new Babylon. From those streets would come the key to the woman to usher in the new age. With the urging of his personal deity, Mumbakata abandoned his practice and began to work with the poorest of the poor residing in New York's five suburbs.

To Mumbakata poverty in New York was by no means shocking. After all he had come from Haiti, the poorest country in the Western Hemisphere. He knew firsthand what it was like to eat mud for survival. These Americans were truly a spoiled group of upstarts. What they grumbled and complained about what would have been welcomed with open arms by his compatriots. Yet for his Mistress' sake the good doctor shifted the focus of his career.

The sacrifice was noticed by his peers and accolades of praise were lavished upon this noble man's crusade to help the impoverished of New York. In fact Mumbakata's fortunes changed drastically for the better. He became a favorite pet of the various philanthropists who frequented the city that never sleeps. Rich people alleviating their guilt would write sizeable checks to the virtuous work. Their kind hearts were rewarded with a tax write off and the feeling that they helped somebody. Recipients that these donors were glad they had absolutely zero contact with.

Of course the good doctor took a heaping portion from the spoils. He had a penthouse apartment and luxuries abounding. His new found fortune, he of course attributed to Nefertiti and her divine guidance. Still there was the perplexing problem of how to find the key to the mysterious woman. His Mistress was vague in specifics but confident that if the search was not abandoned success would be achieved.

Then came a man who was suffering from insomnia. Insignificant in every way by outward appearances. A poor Caucasian male who had squandered his life and living on drugs. Or so, that is what was assumed by the good doctor. All the signs pointed to that after all. Mumbakata in truth did not explore his new patient's past when he discovered the nature of his inability to sleep. A dream of a woman with a black veil. It was the sign foretold by his Mistress, but had the doctor investigated Walter Winimore's past it would have blown his mind. That is if the psychiatrist didn't dismiss the tale as pure delusion.

***

"So you're a C.I.A. agent, Harry?" A.J. asked.

"I know it's hard to believe," said Harold, "but it's true. Now could you please turn on the screen."

"At this point," said A.J. "you should be satisfied with the fact that you haven't any broken bones. I know what you were trying to do with that blow of yours. You were trying to kill me."

"You should learn to respect me then," said Harold.

"Look, don't puff up your chest at me," said A.J. in a very soft but firm voice. "I was an officer in the Green Berets and among other things I have experienced combat. I also have interrogated prisoners." The security chief hesitated. "Is what I am saying sinking in loud and clear?"

"Yes, sir," said Harold. He very much liked to be in the driver's seat. He was comfortable and confident at having the upper hand. Not being in charge was distressing him to the point where anxiety was breaking down his reasoning. He needed to see what has happening to Walter. If Winimore began to talk, the thought frightened the agent greatly.

"Now, why do you want me to turn on that camera so bad?" A.J. was insistent on getting a good answer.

"It's an extremely complicated thing, please turn on the camera."

"No," said A.J. "You have to try to tell me." Then with a slow firm cadence he spoke out. "The camera will not go on until you give me a satisfactory explanation as to why I should turn it on."

"Okay, but you have to swear not to tell anybody," said Harold, "swear by the name of the undying one who sleeps dreaming."

"Damn," said A.J. "This is worse than I could have imagined." The Green Beret thought about his service throughout the Earth especially the Far East. There was one name that evoked terror far more than any other. The soldier had never been convinced that elder gods lurked in the shadows waiting for an opportune moment to return and recapture the world of men. On the other hand it was something he did not dismiss as a fable. Rather than being black or white it was definite gray.

"Swear, by that name we refuse to utter and scarcely dare to speak," Harold was feeling a surge of control and the power gave him a little boldness.

A.J. sat back in his chair and smiled with a grand smile. "I got all the time in the world, don't I?"

"Walter Winimore is a subject of operation NL Premium," the CIA agent spat out.

"Hmm," said A.J. reflexively, "I never heard about that one."

"It's the next generation of mind control. MK Ultra's successor."

A.J. gave out a sigh of frustration, "Didn't you guys learn from Charles Manson not to go down that route?"

"Well that case was an anomaly."

"I do live in New York City," countered the security chief, "don't you think that I know any better?"

"So Walter was extremely hard to mold. In fact it puzzled us to no ends."

"Okay," said A.J. "so you try to brainwash this Walter and you can't do it."

"Right, I won't get into the reasons why now—do to the urgency of time, and the fact that we don't even understand them ourselves. So, since Walter couldn't be brain washed we decided to use his rock solid mind for another purpose."

"And what might that be?" inquired A.J.

"Well you do understand how a telescope works don't you?"

"Quite so, it takes light and then through lenses it focuses it so you can see objects far away as if they were closer."

"Well, Walter Winimore," said Harold carefully, "is our lens."

"A lens to where?"

"To the spirit world if you will," said the agent speculatively, "some other dimension out there. Hell, what do we know?"

"There is more to the story I'm sure," said A.J. with a breath of satisfaction.

"Could we please turn of the camera?" begged Harold.

"Sure," said A.J. Things couldn't be working out better he thought as his finger clicked on the black and white monitor. "What the hell?" he let out reflexively.

"Are you seeing what I am seeing?" asked the spy.

"Yeah, I guess so," said the security chief. He swiftly reached down to his walkie talkie. He lifted the device to his mouth called out, "Code red, code red in unit 356, code red and this is no drill." A.J. rose to his feet. "Come on," he grabbed Harold's suit jacket tugging him, "you're coming with me."

Harold, in disbelief as if waking from a dream, rose from his seat and hastened out the door with the guard.

***

"I am looking at the woman," Walter Winimore.

Doctor Mumbakata's heart was beating overtime with excitement. The long climb was not over but the summit was in sight. "What does her face look like?" It was not a question but a harsh demand.

"There is a black veil covering her features,"

"WELL RIP IT AWAY!" roared the giant.

"Are you sure?" spoke a soft whisper.

"RIP IT AWAY!" came the command.

"Oh my God!" cried out Walter Winimore.

"Do you see her face?" Doctor Mumbakata sensed victory was close enough to smell it.

"Yes," said the man lying on the bed very quietly.

"And what does it look like?" asked the psychiatrist.

140

"It looks like this," said a sweet feminine voice.

Doctor Mumbakata paused. He blinked his eyes over and over to determine that was not hallucinating. Before him sat a woman upon the bed set a woman in black robes. Over her face was a veil.

"Do you want to see my face?" asked the petite woman.

"Yes," came the definite answer.

"Then behold your future," called out the woman. The lady proceeded to lift her hand. Her hand was gnarled with withered skin. She placed it upon her veil. With a fluid motion she tore away the black cloth and her face was exposed.

Doctor Mumbakata stared into the empty expanse before him. The doctor had seen children seared by burning phosphorous. Wounded babies with their skulls blown open and their brains dripping out, but truly in all his travels, Mumbakata had never seen anything as terrifying or disgusting as the sight he saw now. Not only was the wretch's appearance hideous beyond description, but it was a darkness of dread. Light it seemed was sucked into the visage, and then there was the cold. A bitter freeze chilling first the bones of Mumbakata and then permeating to the very soul.

At first Mumbakata was stunned. He was immovable overwhelmed at this unimaginable appearance. Then he rose his massive hand in attempt to shield himself from the gruesome fright that lay before him. In bitter distress the Doctor's heart began to rupture. Mumbakata knew that he was experiencing a heart attack. The pain in his chest caused him to buckle over. Finally the doctor fell to the ground, dead his large hand clutching his broken heart.

***

A.J. and Harold reached room 356. Already there was a flurry of activity like ants on honey was swarming about. Doctor Mumbakata's large body lay on the grown like a fallen tree. Walter Winimore sat snoring on his bed oblivious to what was going on. Next to the bed was the wooden bust of Nefertiti. A doctor was frantically performing CPR upon the psychiatrist. He was pumping his chest with his hands all to no avail. Mumbakata was officially dead, when in truth he died in Cairo many years ago. What was left was an insane husk of a man. Now his body had finally caught up to the head.

***

"Gosh, Bert," said Walter shaking nervously as he lay on his hospital bed, "it's real nice for you to visit me."

The enormous man smiled, "it was that least I could have done for you, Wally."

"Well they say I'll be here for a while," said Winimore.

"I can arrange a trip to another place for you," said Bert, "one where it's a lot more peaceful and quiet."

"Really?" said Walter in excitement, "where is that?"

"The morgue."

Walter felt a strong urge to run away. With a broken leg and a broken arm this was not an option. Winimore did not doubt that the enormous CIA agent would kill him if he so desired. After all it was Bert who was responsible for him being in the hospital in the first place.

"So, Walter," said Harold, "answer all of our questions honestly and nobody gets killed."

"Promise," Walter meekly spewed out the word.

"How did Mumbakata die?" inquired Harold.

"Aw, come on," said Walter, "he died of a heart attack. You know that better than me. I didn't know that he died until they woke me up in the morning."

Harold looked at his partner Bert. The two were Walter Winimore's handlers from the very day he entered NL Premium program. Experience was the best teacher. The large man shrugged his shoulders. Harold to say the least was frustrated. He was watching the events last night in this very room he sat in. Over the camera there appeared a ghostly apparition. Unlike the legends of most phantoms this one shined in darkness. Walter's story was consistent to what Harold had observed. Winimore did indeed sleep through the whole ordeal.

"Well, Walter," said Harold softly, "you get yourself some sleep, why don't you."

The pair rose and headed towards the door.

"Bert," cried a soft voice.

The large man turned around. He was surprised at the soft feminine cry of his name. Upon turning around he saw the wooden statue of Nefertiti still sitting upon the desk next to Walter's bed. In all the excitement it sat idly by. Something about the wooden bust intrigued him. He reached out his massive hand and clutched the bust. "I think I'll keep this."

"Please, Bert- " Walter commenced an objection.

"Do you got a problem with that?" asked the giant agent clenching his gargantuan fist.

Walter sat in hushed silence.

"I thought so," declared Bert and then the pair was gone. The giant of a man leaving with the bust of Nefertiti.

Walter contemplated the recent events. Doctor Mumbakata was dead and he couldn't decide whether that was a good thing or bad thing. With his guidance he had gone to the end of the dream. In doing so he had unleashed a monster into this existence. For the moment his mind was free, but he had walked this road several times before. After the resolution of one vision there came the creation of a new journey. Knowing the source to be the dreams Walter Winimore was confident that it would be yet another nightmare. Yet for Walter to bear the cross of the vision was far better than to startle the sleeping one. For if the elder of dead gods would ever awaken and return to this place, what then? Walter shuddered cutting off that most unpleasant avenue.

Walter chuckled thinking about Bert. Nefertiti always liked a big, strong man. She too, like all the lesser minions of evil and demigods strived to be released into the land of the living. They desired so strongly to mingle with the flesh and blood of humanity. To walk as wolves among sheep. Not to usher in a golden age but to bite and devour. Considering all Walter could not feel the slightest bit sorry for Bert, but even that brute did not deserve the torment and abuse that he would be inflicted with. Through it all, Walter Winimore felt relieved, as if he had a guardian angel watching over him.

***

A.J. the security chief sat watching in wonder on the black and white screen. Walter Winimore was a mystery to him. Through him an old door had been reopened. In his foolish youthful day the green beret desired to be the perfect killing machine. Not only did he tone his body and mind but he explored sharpening the spirit as well. In remembrance he rolled up his right arm. He was drunk in Bangkok on a Saturday night and his buddies gave him a dare. Over the years the vibrant tattoo had faded. The creature once with flashing yellow eyes and breathing red fire head dulled to a pale green. Yet the inhuman head with tentacles of snakes protruding underneath could still be distinctly recognized as to the ancient one who lay in his crypt dreaming blasphemes.

Made in the USA
San Bernardino, CA
06 March 2017